THIS APPEARING HOUSE

ALLY MALINENKO

 KATHERINE TEGEN BOOKS
An Imprint of HarperCollins Publishers

Katherine Tegen Books is an imprint of HarperCollins Publishers.

Library of Congress Cataloging-in-Publication Data

Names: Malinenko, Ally, author.
Title: This appearing house / Ally Malinenko.
Description: First edition. | New York, NY : Katherine Tegen
    Books, [2022] | Includes author's note. | Audience: Ages 8–12. |
    Audience: Grades 4–6. | Summary: "A strange house appears on
    Jac's street on the five-year anniversary of her cancer diagnosis,
    and when she gets trapped inside she will have to confront
    horrors from her past to find a way out"— Provided by publisher.
Identifiers: LCCN 2021058615 | ISBN 9780063136571 (hardcover)
Subjects: CYAC: Dwellings—Fiction. | Fear—Fiction. |
    Cancer—Fiction. | LCGFT: Novels. | Horror fiction.
Classification: LCC PZ7.1.M346972 Th 2022 | DDC [Fic]--dc23
LC record available at https://lccn.loc.gov/2021058615

Typography by Carla Weise
22 23 24 25 26   PC/LSCH   10 9 8 7 6 5 4 3 2 1
❖
First Edition

For Dad

Who taught me that bravery is not all battle and bluster

but is instead gentle and looks exactly like kindness.

I miss you like crazy.

I love you more.

and

To All the Kids That Lived

I see you and I love you.

Tread softly because you tread on my dreams.
—W. B. Yeats

When I was young I lived a constant storm,
Though now and then the brilliant suns shot through,
So in my garden few red fruits were born,
The rain and thunder had so much to do.
—Charles Baudelaire

FOR AS LONG AS ANYONE COULD REMEMBER, THERE WASN'T A HOUSE at the dead end of Juniper Drive—until one day there was.

It wasn't built over time. There were no construction workers, no loud hammering that woke you up in the morning. There was just a cul-de-sac with an empty lot of overgrown grass that edged up against where the woods began. Except now there was a house. It was a wide, windowed structure, larger than the other houses on the street, with steep gables, turrets, and round stained-glass windows in the upper floors. It had all the usual trappings of a house: doors that shut, bricks that knitted together, floors that held you upright, and stairs that guided you from level to level—but it had something more. Something you could only feel.

It had a way of watching you.

It was as if the moment you saw the house, sitting firmly and suddenly there, that the house in turn saw *you*. It watched you through its window eyes, its door like a mouth beckoning you in. *Come a little bit closer,* it said. *Just one step closer.*

And it was in this way that Jac, her bike still braced beneath her, came to see the house for the first time that mid-October day. It was just starting to turn to evening, the sun painting the sky all yellow and pink, a breeze lifting leaves from trees, showing their pale green underbellies. Just another day in suburban New Jersey.

It hadn't been that long since she'd come down to her thinking spot at the end of Juniper Drive: the round, smooth curve of the dead end where she would trace her bike in lazy circles, trying to clear her head. She couldn't clear her head if she was sitting still. The thoughts just buzzed there like angry bees until they threatened to block out everything else. Movement was paramount. It was only on her bike, the sound of the tires zipping along the blacktop, her motions mimicking the circles that birds made in the same pattern above her, that she could finally sort out her thoughts.

She could lay them in clean lines.

Seventh grade and homework and tests and getting through lunch as the new kid.

Also doctors and needles and pills and the knocking that never stopped.

Her mother, worrying and hovering and worrying some more.

Feeling like a freak.

There wasn't much else to say. Five years of pills. Sometimes she imagined all of them—each one she swallowed, that dissolved inside her, flooding her blood system—lined up side by side. Sometimes she glanced up at the sky and thought that line of pills could possibly reach the moon. But that was fantasy and Jac knew it. She was good at math. Three hundred sixty-five days a year times five years is only 1,825 pills. Laid side by side, they wouldn't even stretch across the dead end where she now rode. What felt huge to her was, according to the facts, very little. Sometimes she wondered if that kind of thinking made things worse. She glanced up at the sky and wondered how much the universe cared. Maybe not enough? Maybe too much?

You hear me, universe? she wondered, looking first

at the house that she was certain hadn't been there the last time she'd ridden here, and then up into all that darkness. The stars had just started to wink on like sleepy eyes. Jac imagined a face in the stars, looking down right at her.

Are you listening?

It was always to this cul-de-sac just a few streets down from her house that Jac returned when she needed to clear her head. Which was why she was fairly certain that that house had appeared out of thin air. It had been a while since she was here, maybe a week? Not long enough that she wouldn't have noticed a house where previously there was none. There should have been construction work, boarded walls to keep people out while things were being built. Bulldozers and jackhammers and the steady, annoying buzz of saws. But instead, the house was there, as if it had fallen from the sky.

Jac watched it as she rode her bike in circles, feeling it watching her. She shivered, though it was not cold out, and now, feeling strangely uncomfortable, turned her eyes skyward again, watching the constellations blink at her against the darkening blanket of night. Obviously, it hadn't just appeared. Obviously, it was built, like all things are, and she just hadn't noticed it. Houses, after all, do not fall from the sky.

Jac swept her bike in another clean circle, catching

a glimpse of the side of the house. It was massive and seemed to stretch directly into the woods. Or maybe it seemed to emerge out of the woods. Jac pedaled in a wide, weaving circle again before turning and heading home. It was dinnertime. If she wanted to avoid the nervous worrying of her mother, she'd better not be late. Though, to be honest, avoiding her mother's worrying was impossible lately. Worrying, it seemed, had become her mother's full-time job.

She biked away from the house but couldn't stop herself from glancing back not once but twice more at the dark windows. The house just gazed back at her, windows like unblinking eyes, following her down the street, watching and waiting.

As she rode down the street, she passed Sam Pensky's house. He was her lab partner in biology. Not a friend, so to speak, but friendly. Tonight, Sam and his family were getting out of the car, his father carrying Sam's little sister in his arms. Jac raised a hand to wave, but Sam turned away. A cold feeling pressed against her as she watched them enter their home. She felt strange, like if he wanted to, Sam could see inside her and know the truth. With a shiver, she felt exposed. She wondered sometimes if it was there, etched on her face, everything she'd been through.

When she got home, she stowed her bike in the garage, entered through the basement, and raced up the staircase. She had homework to do and wanted to get a jump start on it before dinner. She didn't make it five steps into the house before her mother's head poked out of the kitchen.

"You okay?" she asked with her forced, unnatural smile. Jac couldn't really remember the last time her mother seemed relaxed. The last time her mother wasn't stretched taut with worry.

Jac held her breath for a second. *Compose your face,* she thought. *Look normal.* She fixed a smile and then turned toward her mother. "Yeah, why?"

Her mother wrinkled her forehead, a question brewing behind her eyes, and Jac knew she wasn't pulling it off. Her face was failing her. She didn't look relaxed enough. She didn't look carefree. She didn't look like a normal twelve-year-old.

Her mother's eyebrows knitted together, her blond curls pulled back with clips, and Jac noticed that there was more gray hair at her mother's temples than she recalled seeing before. "You were out for a while."

"I went for a bike ride," Jac said.

"Alone?"

"Yeah."

"Not with Hazel?"

"Not this time."

"Did you have a fight?"

"Mom! No. He's just busy or whatever." She tried

to keep her voice steady. It always rose when she lied. The truth was that she hadn't called Hazel. She'd wanted to be alone. But that made her mother worry. To her mother, being alone meant something was wrong. And there was nothing worse than that. It meant the world was going to change. Or worse. Being alone meant Jac was brooding and worrying, and lately it felt like there was room in the house for only one worrier. And that person was her mother.

"I just wanted to make sure you were all right," her mother continued. "School okay?"

"It was fine."

"Homework?"

"Math and science. We're doing a geology unit."

"Is there a lot of reading? Because you know the reading—"

"Some," Jac said, interrupting her. "But it's fine."

"Do you need help?" Her mother twisted her hands together, and Jac felt her stomach drop. She was definitely not pulling this off. *Smile!* she thought.

"No way, I got it." Jac grinned and tried to sound breezy.

"Okay, but if you feel dizzy or you get headaches or if you're struggling . . . "

Jac sighed. It was bad enough she needed a tutor and had to take extra-help courses just to keep up with the other kids. Now she had to manage her mother too. The problem was that Jac had trouble remembering things. Facts would just slide out of her mind like magnets slipping down the refrigerator door. It was a side effect, one of the longer-lasting ones, of Everything She Went Through. At least that's what her mother called it.

Never its real term.

That was one of the strangest things she'd noticed about going through something like she had. Some words just lost their meaning, and other words had too much meaning and couldn't be said out loud. Some words, Jac learned, had too much power.

Sometimes her mother called it All of That. Like it was over now. Like it didn't feel just as real and possible now as it had when it happened.

"I'll get you if I need help. I know the drill, Mom. Anyway," she said, trying to tip this conversation in the other direction, "what's . . . for dinner?"

"Pasta Bolognese."

"Sounds great." Jac turned toward the stairs. "I'm going to start on that homework." She took a step forward, misread the distance to the step, missed it, and tripped ever so slightly. She caught the handrail to steady herself, but it was too late. Her mother was already at her side.

"You okay?" she asked, searching Jac's face as if all

the answers were there. As if she could read the future in her daughter's eyes.

"I'm fine."

"Are you sure? Do you feel dizzy?"

"No. I just missed the step."

"Smile."

"Mom, stop."

"Just once."

Jac did, and it seemed to calm her mother down. If she could smile, one of those quick signs that doctors warned her mother about, it meant Jac was capital-*O* Okay. It meant she wasn't sick again. It's funny how a little thing like a smile could turn into a warning that everything was bad. "I'm *fine*."

"I know. . . . I was just . . . " Jac's mother trailed off, her eyes darting around the room, looking everywhere but at her. Jac felt the weight of being capital-*O* Okay hanging all around her. She didn't blame her mother. She understood. She'd read the books. The stories were always the same. Kid got sick; everyone felt bad; kid taught everyone to love in a deeper, more meaningful way; kid died; everyone remembered kid as a hero. That was the only story she had ever known. She'd never read about a kid who'd Gone Through What She Had and lived. They didn't write stories about those kids.

But Jac knew stories shaped things. Without a story, she wouldn't know what would happen next. She wouldn't know how to look life right in the face and keep going. How to survive when she was somehow . . . broken.

Broken.

That, Jac realized was the word. Broken but still here. Broken but breathing.

Some days she would give absolutely everything to just be a kid again. To erase that whole past. To be normal.

"I'm really *fine*," Jac said, just to fill the silence.

"Did you take your pills?"

"Yes." Jac pushed past her mother and started to climb the stairs. "Just like I do every day," she muttered. "Just like I will for the *rest* of my life." She knew it was loud enough for her mother to hear, and to be honest, she wasn't sorry. She took the stairs two at a time, to prove to her mother that there was nothing wrong, that her motor skills were just fine, that her stumble wasn't an indicator that things had gone wrong again. Then she turned in to her bedroom and shut the door.

Jac flopped onto her bed and closed her eyes. She steadied her breathing and listened, waiting to hear the shuffling footsteps of her mother outside her door.

Instead, there was just silence. Jac was grateful for the privacy, something her mother was starting to realize she needed more than most other things these days. She lifted her hand to her chest and laid it over her heart, feeling the steady sloshing of its beat. The calendar on her wall stared back at her as if to remind her it was the middle of the month already. As if she could forget. It was a calendar of elements—each month a new one with facts and figures. Jac wondered what next month's element was going to be, but she had yet to find the bravery to flip the page.

She didn't want to look at the letters that spelled out the name of that month that would mark the anniversary.

Five years.

In her world, five years meant something. It was a marker that people placed on you. A signifier that said if you made it this far, you somehow magically passed *the* test. You were fixed. Cured. That was the word that the world used. But Jac noticed it was never the word that the doctors used.

The doctors said No Evidence of Disease. NED.

She always thought of it like Ned, as in a person. Right now, Ned was her friend, but Jac worried about the day he might not be anymore.

Because the five-year marker was just a myth. It

was random, like the universe. You never know what is going to happen in the next month, week, day, or hour. Her life had been more than just derailed. It had imploded. There was no real way to fix that. She could never go back to who she was before. And she wasn't sure who she was now, going forward.

She thought about that strange house and how it had felt like it was watching her. Like it was waiting for her. She felt the steady thump of her heart, counted to twelve (her favorite number), and then she put on her headphones, pulled out her homework, and cued up her favorite David Bowie playlist.

Yeah, he was old, but there was something timeless about him. Something personal. Like he *got it*. Most days Jac felt like a freak, and David Bowie, well, he was the King of the Freaks.

And he sang all about Five Years. It was one of her favorite tracks from her most favorite album. Bowie understood how it really worked. He was the Starman. He knew that Everything That Happened was all just fate and luck and chaos. He knew staying alive was a chance. Jac had learned the hard way that when something bad happens, if you asked the universe, "Why me?" be prepared for it to answer, "Why not?"

Be prepared for the universe not to care.

2

JAC WOKE THE NEXT MORNING FEELING BETTER. NOT JUST BECAUSE the night had dissolved her worry about things like pills and doctor appointments, but because she woke with a very specific feeling. She woke curious.

And that was something she hadn't felt in a long time.

Where *did* that house come from?

She had to go see it again. Today. Before school.

"Morning," her mother said, passing Jac's door. Jac pulled a brush through her tangled dark hair.

"Morning," Jac said as she went to get her pills from the bathroom cabinet.

"Someone is in a good mood," her mother said.

Jac smiled. She couldn't help it. She was absolutely giddy. Yes, she was definitely going to see that strange house. She went into the bathroom and filled a glass of water, knocking the pills out into her hand. She looked down at them and told herself to appreciate them. The magic that was medicine. The science that happened in her bloodstream.

Today she could, but other days it was hard. Just looking at the pills, Jac was reminded of Everything That Happened. She'd learned that trauma was strange and elastic like that. Out of nowhere it could snap at you, and you'd be back in that fear again. It could trap you, like a spider in amber, and you couldn't escape it.

She tossed the pills into her mouth and swallowed them down with water. She thought of them dissolving, flooding her body, routing out the enemy.

It helped.

"Breakfast?" Her mother popped her head into the doorway.

"Not today."

"Jac, I don't like when you go to school without eating."

"Don't worry, Mom. My so-called *lunch period*"— Jac held up four fingers to do air quotes—"is at ten a.m. That *is* breakfast."

Her mother smiled. It was genuine, and somehow that made Jac feel better.

Remember this, she thought. *Remember moments like this one, when things feel normal.*

Jac got her books together, threw her lunch in her backpack, and kissed her mother goodbye. Her mom glanced up at the clock. "You're leaving early."

"Yeah, I'm meeting Hazel. He's got a test first period, and he wanted me to help quiz him before class."

The lie came quicker and easier than Jac would have wanted. But the nagging, clanking, curious feeling was too strong, the questions too big. Because the truth was, even if she felt bad about lying, Jac needed to see that house again. She needed to know that she hadn't imagined it. And she needed to do it alone. There was no way to explain that to her mother.

She hit the automatic garage door opener and coasted her bike down the slope of the driveway. It was early and the sky was a rich orange, dusted with deep blues. It held the promise of a beautiful fall morning. She sailed down the street, up before anyone else on her block, and then at the bottom of the hill turned onto Juniper Drive. And there, at the start of the street, she hit the brakes.

The house was there. Dark against the woods behind it. Just as massive as before, its windows like eyes, its door like a mouth.

Hello, it seemed to say. *Come closer*, it seemed to beckon.

Jac pedaled down the center of the street. The rest of the houses on this stretch were still sleeping. She stopped her bike in the center of the cul-de-sac.

What are you waiting for? the house seemed to ask. *Come on in.*

Jac tilted her head. She strained her ears. Was she hearing things? Jac pedaled in a circle, watching the house watch her back.

Come inside, Jac, the house seemed to say.

She stopped her bike. This was ridiculous. Houses didn't talk. Her heart beat fast. Was she hallucinating? Hearing things? No. It was just a creepy, empty house at the end of the street. That's all.

She pushed her bike forward and started to ride away. She needed to get to school anyway. But suddenly it was like her bike didn't work. She felt the handlebars wobble and dip beneath her hands, and she hit the brakes hard, panic slithering up her spine. Worry, in a voice much like her mother's, started to chatter in her head.

Jac squeezed her eyes shut.

She had an overactive imagination. That's all it was.

This wasn't any kind of symptom or sign. Sometimes she was worse than her mother.

There's nothing wrong with you, she told herself. She said it again and again.

But she couldn't peel her eyes off that house. That strange, out-of-nowhere house. The house that had just appeared.

She dropped her bike and her bag and marched up the front steps. She was determined to see what was going on inside. In retrospect, it was probably a very bad idea, but Jac wanted to feel brave, so she did it anyway.

When she stepped up to the door, the house seemed to settle. As if it were agreeing with her. She reached for the doorknob and then stopped, her hand hovering just inches from it. It was decorated in an elaborate spiderweb pattern. A bitter cold was wicking off the doorknob, like an ice cube had dropped into her hand.

Just a little closer, the house seemed to urge.

Suddenly the cold seemed to grasp Jac's hand. Her limbs and her belly filled with ice. For a second, she couldn't breathe.

It took a beat and then another before Jac could

move again. She yanked her hand back, as if the cold had turned to flames, and retreated down the steps, two at a time. She grabbed her bike and her bag, and she sped away as fast as she could.

She didn't dare look back.

3

JAC AND HER MOM HAD MOVED FROM CALIFORNIA TO THIS SMALL town in New Jersey at the end of last school year, and now that it was October, she was finding her footing. Her mother had gotten a job as the head librarian of Forest Oaks Public Library, and after Everything Jac Went Through, her mom had wanted a fresh start.

A fresh start was needed after everything fell apart. It started when her hands, seemingly out of nowhere, started shaking. That was the first sign. Then her leg seemed to stop working or her arm started to curl in a way that was strange. It was like her body belonged to someone else and Jac had become merely a puppet to that person. Though to Jac it was never a person.

If there was anyone—any*thing*—pulling the strings, it was a Monster.

Then the tests started and everything fell apart. No, not apart. Away. Everything fell away because suddenly the only thing that mattered was surviving. That's the weird thing about having your life cleaved in half like this. There is the time before and the time after. And the time after will never, ever feel like the time before. In the time after, everything siphons down to a pinpoint.

You only have to survive.

Just survive. Survive the storm. That was how Jac thought of it.

And she did. Jac made it through the storm, but she knew along the way that storm had washed something away. Something powerful and precious about who she was. Something sacred was swept away in all the rain. Something she needed, some kind of truth, that she could never get back.

And because of the storm, it was time for a fresh start.

And a fresh start meant something new, a new coast, a new state. A new life.

New Jersey.

It would have been a lonely summer if it weren't for Hazel. He lived around the corner. He was really into books, and he talked *a lot*. But he was nice and didn't mind if Jac wasn't as talkative, and to be quite honest it was easier that way. He rarely asked about her past, and if he did, he was fine with short answers that didn't lead to more questions. And obviously it was better than being alone. They had spent the summer riding their bikes down to the lake at the edge of their neighborhood. There were fancy houses along the lake, twice the size of Jac's or Hazel's home. Stashed along the docks were small rowboats that belonged to the fancy houses, and one time they stole one and rowed right out into the center of the lake.

Hazel teased Jac that the lake had a monster in it, but she'd just rolled her eyes.

"Monsters aren't real," she had said. "They're just stories."

At the time, Hazel looked less convinced as their rickety little rowboat bobbed on the water, far from the shore. But Jac was fine. She believed in the here and now. In science and math. In what can logically be interpreted. She didn't believe in ghosts or monsters or any of that. She knew what people called ghosts or monsters were just stand-ins for the things they were afraid of. People weren't really afraid of ghosts themselves; they were afraid of the thing that a ghost stood for. A ghost was a question that remained unanswered. And Jac had been given no choice but to look those unknown and unknowable things right in the eye.

She stared them down. She didn't blink. If anyone was a monster slayer, it was Jacqueline Price-Dupree.

That summer afternoon, in fact, she had proved there was nothing to be afraid of when she dived, fully clothed, off the bobbing rowboat and straight into the cold lake. Hazel's shouts were lost to the rush of water and the icy chill across her belly and back. She swam down, her lungs full of so much good breath, her eyes open in the murky lake water. She stared down into the depths of that crater lake and challenged the universe. *Bring it*, she thought, as the breath in her lungs started to burn. *Conjure up your worst*, she demanded. *Go ahead. I dare you.* But nothing swam out of that murky water. Nothing tried to swallow her whole. She stayed down until her lungs, hot and desperate for air, couldn't take it anymore, and then she turned and kicked her way back up to the surface. Jac grabbed the lip of the boat and popped up behind Hazel, who was staring over the other edge searching for any sign of her.

"Boo!" she'd yelled, and Hazel, in shock, tipped right over and went headfirst into the water. When he reappeared a second later, sputtering and coughing, it took only about a moment before he started laughing. Hazel was good like that. He rolled with things. He didn't fight everything the way Jac did. He had an ease about him, a quiet confidence. Hazel's nature was soft, understated, but always there, like a heartbeat. Being with him, she always felt that she could breathe a little easier. Laugh a little quicker. She paid attention to that.

By the time the school year started, Jac and Hazel were tight. She felt braver starting middle school with someone at her side. Not that they were without their problems. It didn't take long for Jac to be teased for her name. Jacqueline had always felt long and cumbersome to her, like an ill-fitting coat with too-long sleeves and misaligned buttons. Jac, on the other hand, fit like her hoodie, snug and warm and zipping up neatly. So that's what she always went by. In her old town, back in California, it wasn't a big deal. But here, in Forest Oaks, New Jersey, for some reason, people seemed to need an explanation as to why a girl had a "boy's" name. Jac found the whole thing to be rather tiresome.

Pair that with Hazel, a boy with a "girl's" name, and the bullies had ammunition for months. Jac blew it off. If she was good at anything it was ignoring the stuff that didn't matter. One positive to come out of going through Everything She Went Through was she learned not to get hung up on small stuff. But she could see it bothered Hazel.

And when they met up for lunch later that day, he seemed off. Jac wanted to tell him about the house, but it didn't seem right.

"What's up, Haze?"

"Nothing," he said, picking around the food on his tray. It looked like meat loaf, but Jac couldn't be sure. Hazel was just messy. His curly hair seemed to refuse the taming of a brush and jutted out in waves from his face.

He pushed his glasses up on his nose and sighed again. He had hazel eyes. The same color as Jac's. It was one of the first things he'd said to her when they met, which Jac found weird. A nice kind of weird, but still weird. She had since learned that Hazel was like this. Kind of weird and kind of messy.

Jac and her mother were unpacking the moving truck, and without even asking, Hazel showed up, introduced himself, lifted one of the many boxes in the truck, and followed them inside. Jac had asked him then if his eye color was why he was named Hazel. It was decidedly *not* why he was named Hazel. In fact, Hazel even pointed out, as he followed Jac into the house, his eyes were brown when he was born. But now he turned those eyes on Jac, and she knew something was wrong.

"Haze, come on. Spill it."

"Nothing."

"You are the worst actor in the world."

"John transferred into my lit class."

"Oh," Jac said. John Johnson had set his scope on Hazel about three weeks ago. Jac could never figure out how a guy with *that* name managed to avoid teasing, though she figured it was all the beating-people-up stuff he did. And for reasons neither Jac nor Hazel could understand, he just really, really liked to torture Hazel. Like some kind of rabid dog with a very big Hazel-shaped bone.

"He asked me in front of the whole class why I had a girl's name."

"Your teacher didn't shut this down?"

Hazel snorted. "Like I can count on teachers. It was Feldman. I think he was napping."

"So what did you say?" Jac asked, unwrapping her sandwich and giving it a sniff. She was concerned her mother had forgotten she hated mayo. She'd been doing that a lot lately.

"I said my mother named me after a rabbit from her favorite book."

Of course you did. There was a beat during which

Jac pursed her lips, nodded her head, and tried to compose her thoughts. "That was *probably* not the best idea, Haze."

"I know! But I panicked. And I'm not good at lying."

"I get that, I do, but . . . is that really something you wanted John, of all people, to know?"

Jac had heard the whole story already. How his mother loved the book *Watership Down*, about a bunch of rabbits trying to find a new warren. She read it twice while she was pregnant and named her son after the main character. Oddly enough, it was one of Jac's favorite books too. In fact, when she'd met Hazel it was the first thing she'd thought of. But not the kind of thing Hazel should have shared with his bully. This could go on all year. But that wasn't something she could tell Hazel. She'd have to say something else. Something helpful.

"It'll die down," Jac said, ditching her sandwich and peeling open her orange. "It always does. And if not, we'll just have to figure out John's most embarrassing secret."

"How are we going to do that?"

"I have no idea. But we will."

She glanced across the cafeteria and saw John sitting with Sam Pensky. John was chattering on, but it didn't seem like Sam was listening as he picked at his food. In biology he'd been totally out of it and barely spoke to her. She wondered about the other night, when she saw him and his family coming out of the car. The way his dad was carrying Sam's sister. How small she looked.

"Something is up with Sam, I think," she said.

Hazel glanced up and then scowled. "Who cares?"

"What do you mean?"

"He's, like, best friends with John. He gets what he deserves."

At the end of the school day, Jac met Hazel in the parking lot by the bike stand, and the two of them zipped through the center of town, dipping their bikes from the road up onto the sidewalk, much to the annoyance of the town's pedestrians. They stopped at Almanti's for a slice of pizza. Jac still wasn't used to how good the pizza on the East Coast was. She had always assumed pizza was universal. Dough. Sauce. Cheese. How terribly and wonderfully wrong she was. After having lived so long in California, she hadn't realized that she was missing out on what really good pizza was like.

"Can you get this everywhere on the East Coast?" she asked Hazel, pinching a gooey slab of cheese off her slice and dropping it into her mouth. It was the perfect combination of sauce and cheese, and her stomach growled like an angry dog. This was the problem with having lunch at ten a.m.

"See, here's the thing," Hazel said, his mouth full of food. He sucked soda through the paper straw. "Basically, you have a fifty-mile radius."

"What?"

"You know a radius. Like a circle. Didn't you learn this in math?"

"I know what a radius is, Haze. I just don't know what you're talking about."

"Okay," he said, picking up the Parmesan-cheese container. "This is New York City. This," he said, moving the red-pepper flakes and the garlic powder around the Parmesan cheese, "is fifty miles around the city. Everything from the cheese to the garlic to the red-pepper flakes is where you can find good pizza. Beyond that, you're on your own."

"What about Chicago?" Jac asked, taking a bite of her crust and wiping her hand on the small paper napkin, which was not thick enough to catch the grease running down her arm.

"*No.* Jac, just no. Look, I understand they think they have good pizza, but that whole thing is a mess. First off, it's upside down. The *sauce* is on top! The *cheese* is underneath. It's like they tried to make a pizza, dropped it on the floor, and then scooped it back up and served it."

Jac laughed. "I'm pretty sure there are a lot of people who would disagree with you."

"That's fine," Hazel said, balling up his napkins and folding his paper plate to put it in the trash. "People can disagree. Doesn't change the fact that they would still be wrong."

Jac paused from cleaning up her plate, locked in a thought, and Hazel, as always, noticed. "What's wrong, Jac?"

It was right there, right on the tip of her tongue. The words seemed to have a life of their own, and Jac had to bite them back. She wanted to tell him about the house. How it had appeared out of nowhere. How she couldn't stop thinking about it. But something stopped her. Something that said that even though Hazel understood everything, he wouldn't understand this. Just like he wouldn't understand her past.

"Nothing. Just brain fog," she said with a laugh. Hazel gave her a small look but let it go.

They cleaned up their things, slipped their backpacks on, and headed out to grab the bikes they'd left leaning against the side of the pizza shop. They biked through town, around two large ponds, sending the ducks into a flying mob of honking feathers. When they got back to Jac's house, they stowed their bikes against the garage and Jac took her house key out. She reached out to slip the key in the lock, and just when her fingers were seconds away from the doorknob, she froze.

The doorknob was cold. The same kind of cold that had seeped from that other house. For a second, she couldn't move.

"You okay?" Hazel asked, giving her another look.

"I'm . . . " But Jac couldn't get the words out. Her brain felt like sludge. The doorknob no longer looked like hers. It had the same spiderweb pattern as the one from the House. That was the way she thought of it now. *House* with a capital *H*. Her hand was starting to shake.

Something was wrong. This was clearly a hallucination. And she couldn't dare think what that meant.

It's a symptom, her panicked mind said. *You're sick again.*

"Jac, you okay?" Hazel's voice sounded like it was coming through a tin can on a string.

And then, just as quickly as it had started, it stopped. The cold feeling vanished. The doorknob was just her regular doorknob. Her house was her house, the light beige paneling, the wide picture window, the wooden slats of her front porch.

"Jac! Hello! You in there?" Hazel practically yelled. "Are you having some kind of stroke or something? Should I call nine one one?"

"What?" Jac asked as the fog lifted. "I . . . sorry. I just . . . spaced out."

Hazel laughed. "No kidding."

Jac swallowed hard and then slipped the key into the lock and opened the door. For a second, she expected to find something wrong. But everything was as it should have been. The house was quiet, the gentle tick of the clock in the kitchen, the lingering smell of the breakfast her mother had made herself before leaving that morning. Couch against the wall. Small upright piano in the corner.

Hazel beelined past Jac, dropped his backpack on the floor, and flopped onto the couch, picking up the remote to turn on the television. He started to tell her a story about something that happened in his math class, but Jac had trouble concentrating. A headache had blossomed in the back of her skull. She couldn't shake what had happened at the door. The House had called to her. That strange, appearing House.

Jac shivered. The floorboards below her feet felt uneven, her steps unsteady. The logical part of her brain tried to warn her. *Pay attention*, it said. *Something's wrong.*

"So, then Mr. Walsh just completely flipped out," Hazel continued on in the background. Every once in a while, Jac tried to nod or mm-hmm so that he wouldn't worry as she walked through the halls and rooms of her house as if she had never seen them before. As if she didn't live here.

Her phone pinged. She glanced down at the screen.

Where are you? Are you home? Is everything okay?

The text was from her mother.

She tapped the screen. **Yes. Sorry. We just got in. Stopped for a slice of pizza.**

The three dots bounced as her mother responded. **Okay. I was getting worried.**

Of course you were, Jac thought as she typed, **Sorry. It's fine. Is Hazel with you?**

Yeah. We're watching television.

Make sure the door is locked. I should be home a little after six.

Okay.

The dots bounced again as her mother typed. **You okay?**

Jac exhaled. It was like some kind of sixth sense. **I'm fine,** she typed. **See you when you get home.**

Okay. Love you. Bye love.

Bye Mom.

Jac couldn't help but smile. Her mother always ended each text message conversation like it was an email or a letter. She always had to formally and officially say goodbye. And she always told Jac she loved her. Jac slipped her phone into her back pocket and flopped onto the couch next to Hazel, yanking the remote from his hand and switching the channel.

"What does that mean?" Hazel asked, pointing to a framed quote. It said:

Sometimes bravery is not
all battle and bluster
but is instead gentle
and looks exactly like kindness

"Um, I don't know. My mom likes quotes."

"But what does it mean?" Hazel said. "Like, what does kindness have to do with bravery? That doesn't even make sense."

Jac shrugged like she didn't know. But she did. At least she thought she did. She thought it had something to do with the way the hero on television, the guy with the sword, might not always be the hero in real life. That maybe being the hero required something softer. That maybe bravery looked different than we thought. But it wasn't anything she could put into words. Not to Hazel.

Not long after six, her mother came home.

"Hey, Mom," Jac said as her mother wearily shed

her jacket and stowed her umbrella in the stand near the door.

"Hey, baby," she said.

"Hi, Mrs. Price-Dupree," Hazel said.

"Hazel, sweetheart, for the tenth time, it's Cynthia. Formal titles give me wrinkles." She slipped her shoes off at the door and rubbed her tired feet. "Everything okay here?"

"Everything's good," Jac said.

"Hazel, you want to stay for dinner?" her mom asked.

"Can't tonight. In fact, I should get home before my mother—" And as if on cue, Hazel's phone dinged. "Speaking of . . . "

Hazel texted her back and then rooted around, collecting his sneakers and jacket. "See you tomorrow."

"Want to bike to school?"

"I can't tomorrow. I have to be in early for labs."

"Okay, see you at lunch."

"Bye, Hazel," Jac's mother yelled from the kitchen.

"Bye . . . Cynthia," Hazel said, making a face at the lack of formality, then pulled the door shut behind him.

They ate blintzes, one of Jac's favorites, and after they were finished, she picked up the plates to do the dishes.

"I got those, Jac. Do you have homework?"

Jac had her back to her mother as she ran the dishes under the water. Her heart thudded in her chest. *Tell her. Tell her what happened. Tell her you saw something that wasn't real. Tell her you heard voices.*

"Is everything all right?" her mother asked.

Jac turned to her, and whatever bravery she had faltered. She looked at the worried line between her mother's eyes. She looked at the face she made. At the years that hung upon her like a mourning shroud. Watching her mother watch her, the way her tired eyes flitted over Jac's face, she couldn't do it. She couldn't worry her. Not yet. Not unless she knew for sure.

"Everything's fine," Jac said as lightly as she could, and then with some playful snark added, "Leave a nearly teenage girl alone." She added an eye roll.

"You've sounded like a teenager for the past two years, and I'm not ready." Her mother got up and laid a hand against Jac's cheek. Her skin felt nice and cool. "Seriously though, you know you can talk to me about anything."

Anything but what I'm currently going through, she thought. "Everything is fine, Mom. I promise."

"Headaches?"

"Nope," she lied smoothly.

"Tremors?"

"No."

"Double vision?"

"Mom," Jac said with real frustration. She hated the checklist of symptoms. Hated the way it felt like everything was just waiting to tip into terrible. Like at any moment it could all fall apart. "I'm *fine*. You have to believe me when I tell you I'm fine, okay? It can't be the end of the world every day."

"Who is talking about the end of the world?" Jac's mother lifted up the dishrag and playfully snapped it at her. "Get that homework done."

Jac sighed and headed down the hall. When she reached the steps, she faltered. Suddenly the carpeted steps vanished and were replaced with wooden slats. When she glanced up, the door to her bedroom was replaced with a wide black front door.

No. Jac squeezed her eyes shut. When she opened them again the steps were back to normal. The door to her bedroom, slightly ajar, was still hers. *Everything's normal.* She said it to herself to see if it felt true. Jac looked down at her hands. They were not shaking.

Everything's normal.

Everything's normal.

Everything's normal.

With every cell in her body she wanted it to be true. Because one thing was for sure; that House, whatever it was, wasn't normal.

36

4

JAC WOKE FROM A DREAM COVERED IN SWEAT. IN IT SHE WAS SUR-rounded by mirrors. One after another, skewed at different angles so that no matter where she walked, she was confronted with her own reflection, over and over again. She couldn't find the exit and she couldn't breathe. The mirrors seemed to loom over her, doubling and tripling until she wasn't sure which version of herself was real—the one looking into the mirror or the one looking back out.

Thirsty and frazzled, Jac reached for her water glass on the nightstand and noticed that it was only three in the morning. Far too early to be up, and yet the idea of going back to sleep seemed impossible. She felt warm, the whole room felt warm, so she slipped out of bed. Her toes dug into the blue shag carpet as she went to her window. She unlocked it and pulled up the pane. The cool fall air whipped around her, blowing away whatever remained of the dream and drying the sweat that had gathered on her skin.

Jac looked down at her hands. They didn't shake. Back when everything went bad, it was one of the first symptoms, so having steady hands became a thing Jac latched on to. Even if she was tripping slightly, even if she was seeing things, as long as her hands were steady, she was fine.

But she knew that hallucinations were a very obvious sign. What else could that have been? What else would make her house feel like *that* House? What else would transform her door into that door?

And then a cold, terrible thought crept up her spine: Was the House even there? Was she seeing that too? Jac pressed the heels of her hands into her eyes until she saw spots. She should tell her mother. She had promised her mother if anything, anything at all, happened, she would tell her, and yet . . . how could she look her mother in the eye and then knowingly, willingly, terrify her? How could she conjure up the nightmare that they had just somehow narrowly escaped?

Five years.

Jac glanced at her calendar. She still didn't have the courage to flip the page. She felt tied to her past, shackled to it. Like she would never get free. Like all she would ever be was the illness.

Stop it, she told herself. She sounded like her mother. There was only one way to figure this out. If the House wasn't real, the only way she would know was to go there. If she went down to the cul-de-sac and physically touched it and felt it, then it was real. She couldn't hallucinate a physical thing. And if it wasn't—then she had to tell her mother that the symptoms were back.

Jac was so very tired of being brave. Warriors. That's what they called kids like her. But Jac didn't feel like a warrior. She felt like a girl that got handed a raw deal. A kid who had something absolutely terrifying happen to her. But also, a kid who made it out the other side.

A kid who lived.

Jac didn't want to be part of the other statistic. But it was always there, lingering like a ghost. Like a threat.

She swallowed hard and stared out into the cool October night. All the houses were shut up tight, lights off. She saw her neighbor's tabby cat slink out of the bushes and across the lawn. It seemed like the only living thing in the world right now.

Except for you, her brain reminded her. *You're still alive.*

Jac crawled back into bed, pulled out her phone, and cued up some David Bowie. She drifted off to sleep thinking only that Hazel would see the House—because he had to—and that somewhere on the other side of the stars, there was a spaceman that made it all okay.

"Lady Stardust," David sang. Jac smiled as she slipped back under the veil.

Still, she slept fitfully and woke uneasy.

But the next morning, a cool October wind came down the street and swept all of last night's thoughts away. She was being silly and, like her mother often said, her imagination was getting the better of her. Houses didn't appear out of nowhere, and they certainly didn't talk. Jac made the choice to put the whole thing out of her head. She was fine. As long as she kept telling herself that, it had to be true.

But then, riding her bike home from school with Hazel, everything went wrong. Her day had been okay. She didn't do great on a test, but she was trying not to worry about it. She was having trouble concentrating on what Hazel was chatting on about next to her when suddenly her handlebars jerked to the side. Before she could stop herself, Jac was thrown like a rag doll to the ground.

"Jac!" Hazel yelled, pedaling over. "You okay? What happened?"

Her knees were burning from hitting the pavement, and the palms of her hands were scraped and beaded with asphalt. Hazel helped her get up.

"What happened?" he asked.

"I don't know. I think I hit a rock or something." The two of them looked back, but there was nothing in the road that would have caused such a fall.

"You sure you're okay?" Hazel asked, his eyes searching her face. She hated the way he looked at her. It reminded her of her mother's gaze. The way it searched her, like headlights, for a truth that Jac was determined to keep hidden.

"Yeah, I'm fine," she said with more bite in her voice than she meant. "I've got to go."

Jac picked up her bike and walked it for a few steps before hopping on and riding off. Hazel called her name but didn't follow.

When she got home, she slipped upstairs to wash her hands. There was some blood, but she was feeling pretty sure she could hide it from her mother when she heard the front door open.

"Jac, you home?"

"Yes," she yelled back. "One second." She cursed under her breath as she heard her mother climbing the stairs and quickly tried to clean up the bloody wads of toilet paper and scraps from the Band-Aids, but she wasn't fast enough.

"What happened?" her mother said, scanning the mess and then scanning Jac. That same look as Hazel, like lamps, giant lights searching for whatever darkness was inside her.

"Nothing."

"Jacqueline. What happened?" She said each word slowly and purposefully.

"I hit a rock or something with my bike, and I fell. I'm fine. It was nothing." Jac tried to move past her mother, but she was blocking the doorway.

"Let me see."

Jac held up her hands so her mother could see. "I'm fine."

"There's blood on your jeans."

"It's from a scrape on my knee. This isn't a big deal."

Her mother chewed the inside of her lip. "How did you fall?"

"I don't know. I just fell."

42

"Were you dizzy?"

"Mom."

"Has this happened before? Put your hands out; let me see them."

"Mom, no!" Jac pushed past her to her room. "Why can't I just be a kid who fell off her bike? Why does everything have to be such a big deal?"

"Because it is a big deal!" her mother yelled as Jac slammed her door.

The next day at school, Jac dropped her art project. They'd been doing a ceramics unit, and she was proud of the bowl she'd made. It was even on all sides with a wide brim, and she glazed it in a brilliant blue, the color of the ocean. It had been perfect for about three minutes before she dropped it on the floor and it broke into three sections. Jac stood over the sections, trying desperately not to cry.

Her art teacher, Ms. Klein, bent to pick up the pieces from the floor. "Oh, that's too bad, Jac. But we can fix it."

The lump in Jac's throat made her voice sound lower than usual. "No, we can't. It's broken."

"Sure we can. Broken things get fixed all the time. Have you ever heard of Kintsugi?"

Jac shook her head. She couldn't pull her eyes off the broken shards. Why had this happened? Were her hands shaking? She thought of the fall on her bike yesterday. The way she'd just lost control.

Broken.

That was the only way she could think of herself.

Ms. Klein got up and pulled a large art book off the shelf of the classroom. Jac could feel the eyes of the other students on her. They watched her like she was a ghost, and Jac wanted to run out of the room.

"See here," her teacher said. "This is Kintsugi. It's a process by which the broken object is repaired with gold, so not only is it fixed, but it's made even more beautiful. It's a reminder."

Jac looked at the picture. The bowls were beautiful, laced with gold like little rivers running through them. She looked at her own broken bowl and felt nothing but despair.

"A reminder of what?" Jac asked.

"That a break is not the end of an object. That repair doesn't restore the object to what it was; it remakes it into something else. Everything breaks. But everything can be fixed. Everything can be remade. There is beauty in the breaking and remaking of a thing."

Jac felt tears well up in her eyes, and she bit her cheek to keep them down. "Not everything can be fixed."

Ms. Klein looked at Jac. There was something there, some sort of understanding. The bell rang, and the other students filed out the door. Ms. Klein shouted instructions for next class. Jac fiddled with the broken edge of her bowl. Why was she so upset? It was just a stupid bowl.

She turned to get her bag when her teacher said, "Jac, before you go . . . I just . . . "

But Jac looked away because there was something too raw in Ms. Klein's eyes. Too real.

"I know things haven't been easy for you. Moving is hard and before that . . . "

Jac shot her a quick look. Did she know? Did all her teachers know? Her heart started to race. Did her mother tell everyone what happened when she was little?

"We all have parts of us that scare us. Parts of our lives that feel terrifying—that we're afraid to face. Parts that we may want to run from. Parts that might feel . . . broken." She laid a gentle hand over the broken bowl. "But a singular event doesn't determine a whole life. Just like a break in a bowl is not the end of that bowl. Healing the breaks, highlighting the breaks, that's where the power is. It's true for bowls and it's true for people. It doesn't need to be something we run from. If you stop running, you'll see that. If you

45

face it, it won't have power over you."

Jac, feeling overwhelmed, grabbed her bag and squeaked out a small, "I'm going to be late for my next class."

She was out the door before she could hear what her art teacher said next.

That night, over a tense dinner, Jac mostly pushed food around her plate while her mother tried to get her to talk. It didn't work, and instead they sat in silence, the ticking of the clock the only sound in the house, until her mother broke that silence with a phrase that chilled Jac to the bone.

"I scheduled a scan."

Jac dropped her fork. Her stomach roiled. "What? Why?"

"Because we need to make sure everything is okay. You haven't been yourself, Jac. You're falling behind in school, you failed another test, you broke your art project, and you've had a couple falls."

"I had *one* fall."

Her mother's lips tightened to a thin line. "Regardless, it's tomorrow, after school. You need to come right home."

5

THE NEXT DAY, AS SHE SAT IN LITERATURE CLASS, STARING OUT THE window, her phone in her pocket buzzed. Jac glanced around the room and then carefully pulled it out of her hoodie pocket. She peeked at the screen.

Hi Honey. Just checking in to see how your day was going.

Of course. Her mother did this at least five times a day. Keeping the phone under her desk, she texted back quickly.

All is fine. In class. Can't talk.

Oops okay. Sorry. Thought you were at lunch. I'll text you later. If you need me, call. Remember the appointment is at 5:30. Come home right after

47

school, okay? Everything is going to be fine.

Jac slipped the phone back into her hoodie just as Mr. Wronski looked at her. "No phones in class, Jacqueline. You know that."

"Sorry," she mumbled.

"You can talk to your boyfriend after class," he added.

Half the class started snickering, and Jac felt her cheeks go pink. *Thanks, Mom.*

She tried not to think about the scan, about the Machine and about how it would change their lives. The very idea of tomorrow slipped away. This happened whenever she had a scan. It was like the next day didn't exist. Nothing existed until she knew for sure if she was okay. She was in limbo. In a nonplace. Like her life was paused until the doctor called and decided her fate.

Jac put her hand over her heart and counted the beats. She tried to steady her breathing.

Even at lunch with Hazel, she still felt like she wasn't really there, still something other than present, still distracted. He kept talking as he always did, but Jac's thoughts wandered past the scan, past her mother's worrying, and back to the House.

What was it about that place that she couldn't stop thinking about it? It was like it had a hold on her. Her fingers itched to open that door, to look inside.

To know what was there.

"You listening?" Hazel said, dropping his sandwich onto his tray.

"What? Yes. Totally." She smiled. "Totally listening."

Hazel sighed. He gave her a look but let it go, just like she knew he would.

When the day finally ended and Jac's backpack was full to bursting with weekend homework, she headed down to the bike rack and found Hazel there already, trying and failing to pop a wheelie. They rode home together, racing down most of the streets. She felt each second going by, each one bringing her closer to the hospital, to the doctors, and finally to the truth. She wasn't ready. She felt it in her bones. She didn't want to know.

And that was when it hit her. There was a solution here. All she needed to do was see if Hazel could see the House. If he saw it, then she couldn't be hallucinating. If he saw it, she *had* to be okay, regardless of tripping or shaking hands. If Hazel could see it, the scan would come back negative.

"Hazel!" she practically yelled. "I want to show you something!"

He gave her a sidelong look, his bike zipping alongside hers. "Okay, weirdo."

"Come on." She turned a hard right, cutting down

the side alley between Poplar and Hickory. The road here was unpaved and her bike rattled below her, shaking her bones. The alley spit them out right at the entrance to Juniper.

When they reached the cul-de-sac, Jac stopped. Hazel hit the brakes next to her. For a moment no one spoke. The two of them just stared down the road. Jac looked from the House to Hazel and back to the House again.

"What are we looking at?" Hazel asked.

No.

Her gut tightened as if her belly were filled with ice. It couldn't be. He had to see it. He just had to!

"Please tell me you see it?" Jac whispered. Her heart thudded inside her, her mind going down all the twists and turns of what it meant if Hazel couldn't see the House. She shivered even though it wasn't cold.

"What?"

Incredulous, Jac pointed down the street. "That!"

"What?"

"The *House*."

"Which one?"

"Are you serious right now? Are you actually serious?" Jac said, cursing under her breath.

"What? Why are you getting so mad? Which house am I looking at?"

"The one that wasn't here a few weeks ago." Jac pointed at the House. It stood just as darkly stoic and serious as it had the other day, the door shut, the windows like big, unblinking eyes. The turrets and gables and the tower on the west side. "The giant House that seems to have grown directly out of the woods. *That* House did not exist a few weeks ago."

"That's not possible," Hazel said. "You probably just never noticed it."

"So you can see it?"

"Of course I can see it."

"That House, right there," Jac said pointing. "You can see that House?"

"Jac, you're freaking me out. Of course I can see the house. But why does it matter? It's probably been there forever and you just never noticed it."

"Never noticed it?" Jac laughed. It was a hard, bitter laugh. A laugh that rested somewhere in the dry valley between relief and tension. *You're okay,* she told herself. *Hazel can see the House, and that means it's real and that you're not falling apart or . . . worse.*

"Hazel, look at it. It's huge. It's a freaking mansion. It's right on the edge of the woods and right in the center of the cul-de-sac. You honestly think I come down here to ride my bike and I wouldn't have noticed a House like that?"

The sun was just starting to dip behind the tree line, and a breeze whipped Jac's hair up. She tied it back in a ponytail. They both hopped off their bikes and walked them slowly toward the House, as if they were drawn forward.

"Houses don't just appear out of nowhere," Hazel said.

"Yeah, I know. That's why we're here."

They were almost right in front of it, guided by some inescapable pull, when a voice behind them called out, "What are you two losers doing here?"

6

THEY TURNED TO SEE JOHN JOHNSON AND HIS FRIEND SAM PENSKY at the entrance of the cul-de-sac. John stood there, arms crossed, hair buzzed like a cadet, so much bigger than the other kids in seventh grade that Jac was sure he'd been left back not once but twice. Sam stood next to him, tall and gangly, his long brown hair tied back in a ponytail.

"What's going on, Bunny Boy?" John shouted.

Hazel cursed under his breath. "What do you want, John?"

"I don't want anything, Bunny Boy. I was just going over to Sam's to play video games and stumbled upon the Losers Club."

"Cool," Jac said. "You can screw off anytime now."

"Your girlfriend's got a bad mouth, Bunny Boy."

"She's not my girlfriend," Hazel said.

"What are you two doing anyway?" Sam asked.

Jac eyed him. Sam had been acting strangely for a few days now, but she certainly wasn't going to bring it up in front of John. Plus, she wasn't sure they were that kind of friends. All things considered, one could say the same thing about her. Still, Jac was good at reading people. There was something in his eyes, something clouding. Something familiar that gnawed at her. Hazel didn't trust Sam because he was friends with John, which Jac totally understood. But for Jac there was something different about Sam. Something that separated him from a bully like John.

"We're not doing anything," Hazel said.

"Sam, that's your house over there, right?" Jac asked, pointing across the cul-de-sac.

"Yeah, why?"

"I got a question for you. This house." She swung her arm up, pointing at the House at the end of the circle. "You see this house?"

John snorted. "Of course we can see it. We're not blind."

"I wasn't talking to you," Jac said. "Sam, you remember it being here last week?"

"What kind of question is that?" John said.

"No," Sam answered slowly, looking at Jac. "I . . . don't actually."

"You have to remember the construction? Must have been loud, right? You're only just down the street. Hammering? Saws? That obnoxious beeping when a truck goes in reverse? Construction workers yelling? Any of it?"

"No," Sam said, looking a touch dazed as he stared up at the House. "I don't remember any of that."

Jac and Hazel exchanged a look before she said, "I told you."

"What are you two freaks going on about?" John said.

"That house," Hazel said. "It wasn't here the other day."

Jac groaned at Hazel's confession as John burst into laughter. "Bunny Boy, I swear you never fail to entertain."

"I'm not kidding," Hazel continued. "Right, Sam?"

All eyes turned on Sam, who stood there, his eyes locked on the House. "I . . . don't know."

John shot him a look. "Dude, what's wrong with you?"

Sam pulled his eyes away from the House and looked at John. His face changed from open and questioning to closed and hard. Suddenly he seemed to have snapped out of whatever trance he'd been in. "I mean . . . I don't know what you two freaks are talk-ing about."

Jac frowned. Apparently, her gut was wrong. Sam was not to be trusted.

"Hey, Bunny Boy, I'll give you ten bucks to go in the front door."

"No way," Hazel said, his hands tight on the han-dlebars of his bike.

"Twenty bucks. Just go and try the door. C'mon, Bunny Boy. You're not a scared little bunny, are you?" John started to laugh. "Can't wait till everyone at school hears about Bunny Boy being a scared little bunny that won't go in the empty house."

Jac looked up at the dark windows, and then she looked at her friend. He was frozen, unable to stand up for himself, and she knew he saw no way out of this.

"Tell you what, John," Jac said, dropping her bike to the asphalt. She shrugged her backpack off. "I don't want the money, but you're not going to bother Hazel anymore."

John laughed. "Your girlfriend needs to protect you."

"I'm not his girlfriend. I'm his friend. And I'll go in there if you leave Hazel alone from now on."

John laughed again, this time harder and crueler.

"Either that or you go in." Jac swallowed. He balked and, in that half second of silence, Jac pounced. "What? You scared? You scared to do something that I'm not afraid to do? Who's the little bunny now?"

John and Sam exchanged a look. "You first," John said.

"You don't have to do this," Hazel whispered.

"I got it," Jac said. "We're ending this."

If going in the House was going to get John off Hazel's back for the rest of this year, it was worth it. Besides, buried under that was another feeling, a softer shivering feeling. She wanted to go in. She needed to go. She needed to know it was real. She turned toward the House, looked at the wide window eyes, the door like a mouth.

She took the steps leading up to the front door slowly, acutely aware of her sneakers connecting with each step, the groan of the wood, her eyes locked on the wide front door. It looked even bigger now that she was nearly there. She reached a tentative hand out toward the fat knob on the door, looking at the spider-web pattern, the one that had appeared on her own door. She paused, her hand hovering just centimeters above the doorknob.

"Go on, then," John yelled. "Don't waste our time."

Jac took a deep breath, steeled herself, gripped it,

and turned. The knob was cold just like last time, but it yielded under her hand. It gave way, a deep click as it disengaged from its latch, and the door swung forward slowly, groaning. A smell reached her, something familiar, something that teased at a memory hidden deep inside her. Something that called to her. She stepped carefully and with purpose over the threshold of the door. She heard it then, music, the sweet low call of the cello, so faint, and then even fainter the high whisper of the violin. For a brief second, she felt like she was floating—out of balance—with the world swirling around her.

She took another step inside. Behind her she could hear Hazel yelling something, but even that didn't matter. She heard only the House, welcoming her, happy to have her here, a warm throbbing beat, as if it had been waiting all this time for her return.

This, Jac thought, *this is the House I've been entering always*.

Yes, the House said. *Finally*.

And then, just behind her, the front door slammed shut.

7

THE ROOM SHE FOUND HERSELF IN WAS ELABORATELY DECORATED, large, cushioned couches and love seats, end tables and hardwood floors. A giant chandelier hung from the ceiling, which seemed to be miles above. A wide staircase to her left led to a balcony that wrapped around the whole room.

And the doors. There were so many doors. She counted a least a dozen on this floor alone, another ten along the balcony. Each with that spiderweb design on the handle. In fact, that design seemed to be everywhere—along the lampshades, embroidered into the cushions, cut into the high glass windows, etched on the lush red wallpaper. In one corner was a grand piano. In the other, a massive organ with three layers of keyboards and black-and-gold pipes.

But the weird part was that everything seemed to be a little bit ruined. There was a cloying, rotting smell about the place, as if water damage and mold lingered in the walls. A large portion of the plaster on the ceiling was damaged and cracking. The air felt thick, almost unbreathable. There was dust on everything; a terrible sense of neglect permeated the space. Jac wondered if she yelled loud enough she could bring the whole thing tumbling down.

Jac walked through the space carefully, tenderly almost, as if she were someplace otherworldly. As she moved through the room, her eyes were pulled toward strange portraits on the walls. In one, something that looked almost like a spider filled half the frame, partially out of sight. In another was what looked like a hoof from a bull of some sort. Then a wisp of white, a dark eye, almost like ghost. The next one was hard to discern, but Jac realized with a sinking dread that it depicted a mouth—a horribly toothless mouth, the gums pocked and swollen. And in the last was a girl, facing away from the artist, her hair cut in a bob, her neck and shoulders slender. There was something so familiar about her that even when Jac heard the low strum of a cello again, she struggled to pull her eyes away from the painting. She glanced around the room. Was someone in here? Jac shivered, though it was not cold. A glimmer caught her eye. On the edge of one of the end tables was a large silver key. It was a skeleton key, with thick teeth at one end. But that wasn't the strange part.

The strange part was that the top of the key was elaborately carved. It showed a face, a girl with long hair and a dark look in her eyes. A familiar look.

With a small gasp Jac realized . . . it was her.

She was sure of it. The key looked exactly like her. As she held it, it trembled in her hand as if it had come to life. Or were her hands just shaking again? She held them in front of her to try to tell. When the door behind her suddenly groaned open, she jumped, dropping the key. It clattered loudly to the floor.

"Holy cow!" Hazel said upon entering. He was followed shortly by Sam and John. Jac, still trembling, pressed her hands together to stop them from shaking. Was she nervous? Was that all it was? Or was this a sign?

Shaking hands is always a sign, her brain said.

"This place is so creepy," Sam said as he and John started peeking around the room. John flopped onto the couch, and a small puff of dust floated upward. Sam tried one of the doors in the corner, but it was locked. Even Hazel pressed down a few times on a single piano key sending an eerie tink, tink, tink into the room. Jac felt overwhelmed with them in here. It was suddenly hard to breathe. Why were they here? This was her place, and now she felt them crowding around her, invading her space.

She shook her head. That was silly. This wasn't her House. She looked down at the key on the floor and picked it back up. Without knowing why, she slipped it into her pocket, suddenly wary about anyone, even Hazel, seeing it. Would they think it looked like her? What could that mean?

Hazel came over to her. "You okay?"

"Yeah, I'm fine."

"This place . . . it's a lot. What is that smell?" Hazel asked, wrinkling his nose. Jac smelled it too. It was biting, strangely antiseptic, as if the whole place had been washed down in bleach, which, considering the state of the House, didn't seem possible. It passed over them like a wave, and then the smell vanished.

Like some kind of ghost.

"Come on, losers," John said, getting up off the couch and opening one of the doors. "Let's see what we can find."

Jac's stomach went tight as she watched him pull out his phone, turn on the flashlight, and point it toward the darkness behind the door. There was something unsettling about it. Like they didn't belong here. Like they shouldn't be looking.

And as if the House agreed somehow, within a few seconds John let out a terrifying scream. It was not a fake scream. It was not a joking scream. It was not a fooled-you-and-made-you-jump scream. It was real, and it came directly from terror that had been torn from the pit of his stomach.

Sam and Hazel and Jac ran over to where he was standing. The light from his phone showed what looked like a kitchen. There was a table, split in two, lying broken on the floor. In the corner was a fridge, the door of which was partially open. Something rancid oozed out of it. In the corner was a rusted sink, the pipes exposed. As with the front room, everything was coated in dust.

"Something . . . something was there," John said, his voice shaking.

"What kind of something?" Jac asked.

"I don't know. It was small."

"Probably a rat," Hazel offered.

John turned on him, his voice a growl. "It wasn't a rat. You think I would be worried about a rat?"

"Leave Hazel alone," Jac said, and to her surprise, John did. Instead he kept his eyes down as if afraid to look up and ran his hand over his shorn hair.

"Tell me what it looked like," she said as evenly as possible.

"It was small, like the size of big cat or a small dog. But it didn't walk on four legs like a normal animal. It sort of . . . scuttled, like an insect or a spider. It was right there," he said, pointing toward the half-open refrigerator. The kids held a collective breath as John lifted the light again and shone it toward the refrigerator. The wallpaper was peeling, causing a shadow near the back of the fridge. Jac watched it, unblinking, once again willing something to show itself, like she did that day in the lake. Maybe Jac was ready to see a monster after all.

Which was good, actually, because something, *something*, stretched what looked like a thin, long gray finger out from within the fridge. It clutched at the door as a few more fingers followed, just as long and just as gray with cracked, blackened fingernails. Something wet dripped from the fingertips. They could have been human fingers, but they were longer, distorted.

All at once everyone started screaming. John dropped his phone, and Sam and Hazel pulled him back as they slammed the door shut and held their weight against it as if that would stop whatever was in there from coming out.

Jac's hands started to shake.

"Did you see that thing?" Sam asked, his breath coming faster. "Someone tell me you saw that thing."

"We all saw it," Hazel said. "And now I think it's definitely time to get out of here."

Jac felt the weight of the key in her pocket. She looked around the room again, at all the doors and the layers of dust. What was this place? This out-of-nowhere House? This House that had just appeared?

The more she looked, the more rot she saw. The walls were cracked wood, paint peeling from what looked like water damage. The windows were blacked out. The smell of mildew sat heavy like dank breath. Suddenly, as if there were a leak somewhere, the plaster of the ceiling started to peel and drop to the floor. The scent of rot behind it was stronger now. Like the House was decaying around them. It was cold and she shivered, feeling queasy.

And something living was just on the other side of that door.

"Come on," Hazel said. Neither Sam nor John argued with him. It was only Jac who suddenly found her voice, after her hand slipped into her pocket to clutch the key.

"Wait," she said softly. They stopped and turned

toward her. Sam and John gave her an incredulous look. Hazel stepped forward, and his eyes offered something softer. Something like an answer.

"We *need* to get out of here, Jac," he said. He had a look on his face, something close to begging.

She looked down at her hands and watched them shake. She didn't bother to hide it. She knew Hazel was right. She should go. She should go and never look back, and yet something was keeping her rooted to this spot. Something inside told her there was more going on here than she knew. And that somehow, she needed to figure this out.

Something told her that key in her pocket was for her and her alone.

"I just think we should see what's going on."

"What's going *on*?" John said, his voice going high as he repeated and mocked her. "Are you kidding me?"

"Jac, I really don't think it's safe," Hazel said.

Before Jac could respond, a loud slam made them jump. Their eyes tracked up slowly to the balcony, where a door swung, like it had just been opened.

"Yeah, I think maybe it doesn't want us in here," Sam squeaked out.

"I'm out," John said. "And you're all idiots if you don't come with me."

He headed toward the front door, followed quickly

by Sam, and then Hazel, and finally a reluctant Jac. The keyhole of the front door cast just the tiniest bit of sunlight through it. They were leaving, and part of Jac's brain understood that was smart and safe because there was something in this House, something strange, something probably dangerous. But the part of her brain that thought this was being drowned out by the part that told her to stop, to wait. To just think about it. The part that wanted to open that kitchen door and look into the fridge one more time.

John yanked opened the door, and the bright light of outside filled Jac's view. Before she even had a chance to think, Hazel grabbed her hand and all four of them barreled through the front door.

But there were no birds, no orange light of the setting sun. No deep woods. No cul-de-sac. No bikes left haphazardly on the side of the road. The door they stepped through—the one that should have taken them outside—instead led back into the parlor. They were standing in the same spot, the front door across the room once again.

"What the . . . ," Hazel muttered.

"I don't understand," Sam said.

John, angry now, ran through the parlor again, yanking on the front door, but as soon as he stepped through, he was back in the parlor, appearing behind them through another door like some kind of loop. "This isn't possible," he said, and charged at the door again, this time faster, as if brute strength alone could beat whatever was happening in this House.

When he came back through one of the other parlor doors, John's breathing was getting hitched. "Okay," he said. "There's got to be some explanation. Another door. Another exit." He bolted up the balcony steps and stopped at the first door, the one that had creaked open. He lifted his phone to shine a light in.

"Guys, this is it," he yelled down to them. The trio watched him from below. John leaned on the balcony, calling down to them, his voice light and hysterical. "This one leads out."

"How?" Sam asked quietly. "How can we get outside from the balcony? That doesn't make any sense."

Hazel and Jac exchanged a look before shifting their eyes to John.

"Come on, guys!" he yelled, his voice going higher and lighter as if he'd inhaled helium. "Let's go." He waved his arm at them, beckoning them to come up. Something cold passed through Jac. Something was wrong. Sam started toward the staircase, and Jac grabbed his arm.

"Don't," she whispered.

John stood on the balcony in front of the open door,

its darkness framing him. They could only watch with horror as, from that darkness, long, thin gray fingers appeared behind John's head. They stretched out of the dark, wet hands on the ends of impossibly long arms. And as they watched, someone—some*thing*—grabbed John Johnson and dragged him into that dark room, the door slamming tight behind him.

They heard his scream for just a moment before it, too, was swallowed up, and then there was nothing.

8

THERE WAS A BEAT AND THEN ANOTHER. FOR A SECOND NO ONE moved. There was nothing but panicked breaths as they all stared up at the dark wood of the door that John vanished behind; that impossible, terrible door. Then with a small cry, something just above a whimper, Sam raced up the stairs and grabbed the handle, pulling on it so hard that Jac didn't understand how the screws could possibly still hold.

But it didn't open. He banged on the wood, screaming John's name. He pulled again and again at the handle, but the door, like a cruel secret, refused to yield. He was yelling so much that it took Jac a second to realize there was another sound underneath it.

A keening sound. A cry.

No, not a cry.

A shriek.

"Sam, stop!" she yelled. Once he was quiet, they could all hear it. It was like a wail at first, but now the pitch went up, louder and sharper, until it was ear-splitting.

Was that John? Jac thought, her stomach rolling. And if it was, what was happening to him?

"What is that?" Hazel whispered next to her.

"I don't know," she said. *It can't be John*, she thought. *It can't be . . . human.* She thought of long, gray, wet fingers, and she swallowed back a wave of nausea.

Sam backed away from the door, stepping gingerly down the stairs as if whatever was screaming—that nonstop screaming—wouldn't notice him if he moved softly enough. He joined Hazel and Jac, and the trio huddled together, stepping backward, no one daring to look away from the door that John had disappeared into. It felt like if you took your eyes off it for a second, whatever snatched John away would take you too.

As if you were nothing.

The screaming was clawing its way into Jac's mouth and ears and nose, filling her like a poison. When it stopped, it felt like someone had lifted a record needle. The relief was everything. She inhaled deeply just to be sure she still could.

"We need help," Sam whispered.

Help? The word felt weird in her mind. Who could possibly help them here?

"We *need* to leave," Hazel said, his voice hitching. He bolted for the front door and, like last time, wound up coming out one of the other doors, this time on the balcony. Jac's heart fluttered in her throat. What if whatever got John got Hazel? What would she do?

"Hazel, come down," she said.

"We're trapped," he said, his voice going high and light. *Just like John*, she thought. What if the creature fed on their fear? What if that was how it found them? What if it just waited until their fear was so great and it used that to track them through the House?

"We're trapped," Hazel said, his voice raspy, "and we're never getting out. We're going to die."

"Come down. It's not safe by those doors," Jac said.

Hazel hazarded a glance back at the door and then scurried down the stairs and joined Jac and Sam on the ground floor. "What are we going to do?"

"Let's call someone," Sam said, and at the idea of getting help, Hazel immediately perked up. He reached into his pocket and pulled out his phone.

"Who are you calling?" Jac asked.

"The police," Hazel said. "My mother. Someone. Heck, anyone."

Jac could hear the ring, small and tinny, coming from Hazel's phone. When it stopped, Hazel hit speakerphone. "Hello? Hello? Can you hear me? Hello?"

There was a pause, and then they heard Hazel's voice echoed back to them through the phone. "Hello? Hello? Can you hear me? Hello?"

"What the . . . " Hazel held the phone away as if keeping it near him was dangerous. Jac and Sam listened to the mimic of Hazel's voice repeating the message over and over again, each time, the voice getting a little higher, a little more hysterical. It pinged back and forth, faster and faster, a distorting echo, until it morphed into a maniacal laugh.

"Hang up," she whispered.

Hazel stood there, his hand shaking, staring at the phone.

"Hazel, hang up the phone," she said again.

"That's . . . that's my voice. How did they get my voice?" But then the laughter changed, and it because a scream. It was the same shriek they'd heard earlier, when John had vanished.

Jac snatched the phone from his hand and ended the call.

"What is happening?" Hazel asked.

"I don't know. But I do *not* think we want whoever or whatever that is to find us."

"Jac," Hazel said softly, as if he feared the House was listening. "How did it get my voice?"

"I don't know. It's the House. It . . . I don't think we should try to contact anyone outside. I don't think that's an option anymore."

"How do you know this?" Sam asked, turning a dark look on Jac. "How do you know so much about this place?" He took a step back, his fear hitching dangerously close to panic.

He's just scared, Jac told herself. *Just keep him calm.* "I don't know anything about it, Sam. It's just a feeling. That's all. I just don't think we're going to be able to get out with outside help."

"So how do we get out?" Sam asked.

"Yeah," Hazel added. "How do we get out?"

Jac felt the pressure of the key in her pocket but said nothing. "There has to be another door. Or a window. Something."

"The front door," Hazel said, pointing, "doesn't lead out, so what does it matter? We're trapped."

"We're not trapped."

Hazel snorted. "Are you serious? Don't kid yourself. We are *trapped* in this house."

"I think it's important we stay calm."

"*Calm?* How can we possibly be calm? We're trapped in a creepy trick house with some kind of *thing* in it, and that *thing* just took John. It just took him!"

Jac strained her ears. Was the shriek starting again? Was it responding to Hazel's fear? "Hazel, I need you to keep your voice down if you don't want that *thing* to find us." She didn't share her theory about fear. It was better to let him think that the creature could just hear them. That was far less terrifying than the possibility that fear was the way she found them—yes, Jac already thought of those wet gray fingers as belonging to a she—that fear was how she tracked them like some kind of ghostly sonar. Because if Jac was right, if fear was what that creature hunted, Hazel would certainly be next. Then probably Sam.

And that left Jac alone in this House.

"Look," Sam said, holding up two hands. "You left your bikes out there. Eventually someone will see them."

Hazel perked up a bit. "Yes! Our backpacks. My school ID is in it. When I don't come home for dinner, my mom will call the police. It's only a matter of time before they start talking to the families on this block. Before someone notices this house. Before they figure it out. The police will talk to everyone on the block and see if they saw anything."

Jac sighed. "But no one else was on the street with us. No one saw us come in here."

There was a pause, and then Hazel shook his head. "Someone is going to come help us."

The ice sloshed in Jac's belly again. For a brief moment she wondered if he was right. What would happen when the police came to this street? "I don't know, Hazel."

"What is with you?" Sam snapped.

"What?"

"All you're doing is making the case that, what? That we're . . . stuck forever. That we're going to die?"

Die.

Jac took a deep breath. "No, I just don't think we should wait on anyone else. I think waiting makes it much more likely that she . . . that that thing . . . will find us. I think we need to find our way through this. I think we need to figure out how to get out."

"How?" Hazel asked.

"I don't know. We can't go back out the door, so maybe we've got to go through the House. Maybe the only way out is through."

"Through which door?" Sam asked. "The one that John disappeared into? You want to take that chance?"

"Whatever that thing was that took John, it took

him somewhere," Hazel said. "I don't think we should go looking for it. I think we should stay here and wait for help."

"But what if that thing comes looking for us?" Jac asked softly. Hazel didn't meet her eyes. "What if there is no help? What if that thing is the only thing that is coming?" As she asked these questions, her hand went to the key in her pocket.

Sam narrowed his eyes. "What is that?"

"What?" she asked, her voice rising. "Nothing."

"What do you have?" Sam asked.

Jac hesitated and then exhaled. There was no point in hiding it from them, and truthfully, she probably wouldn't be able to. The desire to hold the key was strong. It seemed to sing in her pocket. She pulled it out and showed them.

"What is that?" Hazel asked, plucking it from her hand. "Where did you get this?"

"It was on that table," she said, pointing at the dusty end table, "when we came in."

Sam gave her a look and then said to Hazel, "Let me see it." Hazel handed the key over, and Sam held it up in front of Jac. His eyes went as wide as saucers. "Why does it look like you?"

"Whoa," Hazel said, just now noticing.

"I don't know," Jac said.

"You don't know?" Sam asked, his voice getting hard. "You don't know why there is a key here that looks exactly like you? You . . . " He paused and then looked from Jac to Hazel and back again. "Wait, is this a prank?" Sam asked. "Did you guys set this up to mess with John? To mess with me?"

"No, Sam, I swear we didn't," Jac said. "We don't know what is going on either."

"Honest," Hazel added.

"Is this 'cause John was teasing you?" he asked, turning toward Hazel. "Is this how you get him back?"

It hadn't happened yet, but Jac had the distinct feeling that in his fear, Sam's hands were about to curl into fists. She stepped between the boys.

"Sam," she said as calmly as possible. "This is not a prank, and if it were, it's way over our heads. There is no way we could pull this off. I know it seems impossible that these things are really happening—that John is missing, that there's some kind of creature in here, that we can't . . . get out—but that is the truth. And we all need to stay as calm as possible and figure this out."

"Calm?" Sam barked. "You expect me to stay calm?"

Jac strained her ears and was sure somewhere she heard the cry start up again.

"Yes, Sam. I need all of us to stay calm so we can figure this out. There is a way. There is always a way. We just have to find it."

Sam looked at her for a beat and then over her shoulder at Hazel. His face was an unreadable mask. "Here," he said, tossing the key at Jac's feet. He turned and walked away from them, heading toward one of the doors.

"Where are you going?" Hazel asked.

"I'm finding a way out," Sam said, before turning to them and adding, "before it's too late."

9

HAZEL AND JAC FOLLOWED SAM AS HE TRIED EACH DOOR AND FOUND it locked. With each tug on the handle, Jac's stomach dropped a little more. They were all thinking it. They were trapped in this room, but no one dared to say it. Door after door after door refused to yield. Was she wrong? She still felt it, deep inside her, this idea that they had to go through the House to get out, but with each locked door she second-guessed herself.

"Maybe the key," Hazel offered as Sam reached the last door left. It was the one that led to the broken-down kitchen, the one where they'd first seen those long gray fingers, and the one no one wanted to open. So naturally, once Sam touched it, it creaked open with a slow, menacing groan.

The trio stopped and stared, hovering, each waiting for one of the others to take that first leap and step over the threshold.

As Jac stood there, staring into the dark of that room, she couldn't help but think about the way the House pulled at her, the way it woke her from dreams, the way it seemed to speak to her. She knew, without knowing how she knew, that it *must* be her that took this next important step. If the three of them were going to leave the parlor, they were going to do it following her.

She pulled her phone out of her pocket and turned on the flashlight. She swept the light across the room, pausing at the fridge as they collectively waited for whatever had been there before to reappear.

They waited a beat, and then another. The room was still. The only movement was her beam of light, reflecting off the dusty surfaces.

Jac stepped over the threshold. The tiles on the floor felt soggy and gave slightly under her weight. She stepped gingerly, suddenly afraid the space might not hold her, let alone the rest of them.

"Be careful, guys," Jac said. "The floor feels . . . weird." *Wrong.*

Hazel and Sam followed her into the room, the

light on their phones also sweeping the space. There was no sign of those long gray fingers, and for that they all let out a collective breath. But Jac was going to check out the whole room before she decided it was safe. When she turned to look back at the door they'd walked through, her light shone across something written on the wall. As she read it her hands shook so badly, she dropped her phone, a small gasp escaping her lips.

Hazel and Sam spun around and shone their lights on the same wall. Written in what she hoped was just red paint, it said, *The House You've Been Entering Always. Welcome Home, Jac.*

Her head swirling, she reached down and with shaking hands picked up her phone.

"What does this mean?" Hazel said. "Why is your name on the wall?"

"I . . . I . . . ," she stammered before falling silent.

"Yeah . . . and why does that key look like you?" Sam added.

In her confusion and fear, Jac chose to ignore the bite in his voice. "I don't know." But she heard it in her head, that voice, the voice from when she'd first approached the House, telling her to come closer, to come inside. The voice she was sure was a symptom. What could this possibly mean?

Hazel snapped a picture of the writing on the wall. "Why did you do that?" she asked.

"Evidence? I don't know. It's just very weird that your name is on the wall. I feel like you're being . . . targeted or something." Hazel wouldn't meet her eyes. He turned back to the wall. "And what does *The House You've Been Entering Always* even mean?"

"I don't know." A headache unfurled behind her eyes. It hurt to look at her name up there on the wall, for everyone to see. She felt raw and exposed. "Let's just try and find another way out, okay?"

Sam gave her a pointed look but said nothing. They swung their flashlights around the space and found a small half door at the back of the kitchen. Jac glanced once more at the message on the wall. The handwriting, which was shaky, looked strangely familiar. With a sinking stomach, she started to think it looked like her own.

No, she thought, shaking the idea out of her head. *You're just getting spooked; that's all.*

They reached the door and it creaked open.

Unlike the previous room, this one was awash in light. It was a long, narrow hall, still dusty, and heaped full of . . . things. Jac wondered if it was some kind of storage space. There were piles of broken furniture here and there. Dressers without drawers looking like faces with open mouths. Nightstands, mattresses up-ended, stained and foul smelling. The antiseptic smell was strong here, burning Jac's nostrils.

"Oh, that smell is awful," she whispered.

"What smell?" Hazel asked, loudly enough to catch Sam's attention. He turned and gave her another long look.

"You don't smell it? I could smell it in the parlor too, but it's much stronger here." She sniffed the air again. "Like bleach, like . . . "

A hospital, her brain offered. She shoved the thought away.

"Like the tip of my tongue feels numb. And my nostrils are burning. You guys really can't smell that?"

"Is that another door?" Sam said, pointing down the hall.

"Yes!" Hazel said, and the two of them took off. Jac was left behind, wondering how it was possible they couldn't smell it. As the boys gained distance going down this long hall, she called, "Hazel, wait for me."

"Come on, Jac; I think we found another door."

The hall bent, and Jac started to feel a little dizzy. It felt almost as if the floor was pitching at a strange angle. She felt unsteady on her feet. What was hap-pening? As she passed a stack of mattresses pressed against the wall, one of them started to tip onto her. She yelled, tried to push it away, and fell on the ground. She was pinned for all but a second before wriggling out. She was about to call for Hazel when something caught her eye.

It was a bed. Not like a regular bed, but one with railings on the side and buttons that go up and down. The kind they have in hospitals. Her breath caught in her throat.

As she got closer, there was a low, urgent knocking sound, steady, determined, like something demanding to be heard.

"Hazel!" she yelled. She could hear him faintly yelling her name. The bed seemed to beckon her as she kept taking one tentative step after another.

The knocking was getting louder. *Insistent* was the only word Jac could think of. She couldn't pinpoint where it was coming from. It sounded like the wall but also the ceiling, and for a moment it felt like even the floor vibrated under her sneakers. With each bang, Jac felt herself flinch, but she continued to move forward, as if she couldn't stop herself. As she walked, the knock moved with her, mimicking her footstep. She was just at the end of the bed when she saw there was a clipboard hanging there.

There was writing on it, and for a second Jac was sure she knew what it was going to say.

No.

She didn't want to look, and yet her stomach flipped over as her hand just kept reaching for that clipboard. She couldn't stop it if she wanted to.

She heard Hazel yell her name, but she couldn't take her eyes off the bed.

The hospital bed, her brain said. *Call it what it is.*

She thought of the graffiti welcoming her home. The way the House called her. The key that looked like her. There was another loud knock. Then another. Then another. Faster and louder until the knocking grew in volume and repetition, the banging coming faster until Jac swore she couldn't tell if it came from the walls, the ceiling, or the floors. Or inside her head.

In the distance she heard yelling. "John!" Sam yelled. "John, is that you?"

The banging had reached a crescendo now, and Jac looked at the bed. For a split second she was sure someone was in it. Someone small. The sheets moved, and she recoiled as something gray and shadowed, something terribly insect-like, scuttled out from under the covers and slipped behind a nearby dresser. Seeing it, a sickness spread through Jac. She did not know if it was the thing that had taken John, but she did not want to find out.

Go get Hazel, her brain said. She turned to go, but

the clipboard was still in her hands. She brought it forward, her heart skipping and tumbling inside her.

Suddenly the knocking stopped. The sudden silence was enough to freeze her. But it lasted only a moment.

It was followed by a blast like an air horn, and, terrified, Jac dropped the clipboard and fell to her knees, her hands covering her ears. The knocking returned, making the walls shake, and she braced herself for another blast of painful noise.

She opened her eyes long enough to look down at the clipboard, to read what was written there, what she knew in her heart of hearts would be written there.

Name: Price-Dupree, Jacqueline

Age: 7

Status:

After *Status* there was just a hard dark scribble, as if whoever wrote it didn't want her to know. Tears filled her eyes, blurring out the rest of the form as the blast of the air horn sounded again, rattling her bones.

Jac knew this sound. She had heard this sound every year for five years. It was the sound of unknowing. The sound of uncertainty, the moment when your life could tip into horror or keep going like everyone else's. The sound was a line in the sand. A possibility of finite days.

A possibility of death.

No, please no.

It was a sound she was supposed to hear on this very day. Her mother had scheduled the appointment for the MRI scan. And this was how it sounded, every time. Jac felt the knocking down in her bones. She leaned forward, tucking into herself as if she could somehow get so small that she would mercifully disappear. Her head felt like it was floating a million miles above her. And then everything dissolved into that first terrible memory.

She was seven years old again.

"Remember what we talked about?" Jac's mom said, smoothing back her hair.

"Yes," seven-year-old Jac said, fiddling with the action figure clutched in her hand. "It's going to be loud but it won't hurt."

"That's right. And it's okay to be scared."

"It's okay to be scared," Jac whispered.

"Mommy gets scared too, but then she remembers that this will only help us get you better."

"I know, Mommy," Jac said. Her mother was gripping her hand so hard it was starting to hurt, but Jac was afraid to let go. Afraid of what would happen if she let go.

Afraid that if she let go, Mommy might never hold her hand again.

When the nurse appeared, Jac started to cry a little, the tears bubbling out of her before she could stop them. She didn't want to go into the tube or wear the thin little gown. She didn't want to go into the cold room and lie so still that she felt like she couldn't breathe. And she didn't want to hear the noise. The banging knocking and then the horn blast. Still so loud even through the squishy foam earplugs the nurse would press into her ears.

"Are we ready, Jaqueline?" the nurse asked. She was tall and thin with a narrow face that reminded Jac of a bird. But not a friendly bird. A mean bird. A hawkish bird with a hooked beak. A bird that would peck at her until there was nothing left. She was a stranger. Only strangers used Jac's full name. Inside her, Jac felt something harden.

"Okay," Jac's mom said, squeezing her hand and swiping at a tear on her face. And just like that they were up and out of those plastic bucket seats and crossing the room. Jac willed her feet to move slower but they marched on, betraying her, as she was guided by her mother into what she thought of as the Cold Room.

In it was the Machine.

"Remember I'm right here, okay? I'll be on the other side of the window, but I'll be able to hear you, okay? So if you need me, you just say so."

"I'll be fine, Mommy," Jac said, as a single tear slipped down her cheek.

"It'll be over soon. And then we'll go get some ice cream, okay?"

Jac nodded. She didn't want her mother to know that even ice cream tasted funny after being in the Machine. Nothing felt right afterward for days. Even Mommy wasn't right. Not until the doctor called and told her what happened next. Jac wasn't sure which part she hated more. Being in the Machine or the weird in-between time that followed when they waited and late at night, she could hear her mother crying so hard. The sound of her mother crying terrified her. Terrified her even more than the Machine and the waiting.

She understood that she was sick and that this was going to help her get better. That there was something inside her that they needed to get rid of. Something that could hurt her, but the doctors were going to cut it out and then it would all be fine. She tried not to think about that part.

The nurse led Jac toward the Machine. She helped her climb up onto the cold, thin plastic tray. From her point of view, it was like lying on a giant tongue, which would slide right into the Machine's mouth. Jac squeezed her eyes shut. *Don't think about being eaten.*

Don't think about being eaten. As the tray jerked backward, pulling her into the tube, Jac tried to not think about any of it. She tried to think about dogs and kittens, her favorite television shows, and summertime. But most of all she tried not to think about how tiny the tube felt. How if she moved her arms or legs at all, she knew she would bang into the sides or the top. How it felt like she was trapped in this Machine, trapped in its mouth. She squeezed her eyes shut. She tried not to think about how she was being swallowed by it. How she would be chewed up and disappear forever.

"Mommy?"

"I'm right here, baby." She heard her mother's voice through the speakers. "I'm right here. This is all going to be over soon."

"Are we ready to get started?" the nurse asked.

Jac nodded and then remembered they couldn't see her. With a shaking voice she said, "Yes."

And then the knocking started. It sounded so loud, like someone was banging on her skull. Jac squeezed her eyes shut and tried to breathe against it. *You're okay*, she told herself. *You're okay*, she said again as the air horn blast made her jump and two fat terrified tears slid down her cheeks.

"You're okay," she whimpered.

"Jac, wake up."

"Jac!"

The voice came through tinny and warbled, but Jac blinked her eyes open and Hazel and Sam were standing over her.

"What . . . what happened?" she asked, pulling herself up off the filthy floor. "What was that noise? Like an air horn?"

Sam and Hazel exchanged a look before Hazel said, "An air horn?"

"You didn't hear it? And the knocking. It was so loud; the walls were shaking. It was . . . " She trailed off, looking at their faces. Hazel's was all concern, but Sam's was something else. Something distrustful.

"We heard a few knocks on the other side of this door we found, but it wouldn't open. I thought it was John. That's it. Nothing was shaking the whole room," Sam said. His look darkened, and in it Jac could see that he still thought she was keeping secrets. And he wasn't wrong; they just weren't the secrets he was thinking of. "And you were nowhere to be found, and now here you are, sort of just passed out. Did something happen?"

"I . . . " Jac got up, brushing off her hands and her knees. She remembered the clipboard suddenly, but when she looked it wasn't there. Neither was the bed.

Had she imagined them? She thought of the thing that lay in the bed and shivered.

"What's going on, Jac?" Hazel said. "Why were you all the way back here?"

"I thought I saw something."

The memory of her past lingered around her. She could smell the antiseptic odor of the Cold Room. She could still hear the blast of the air horn and the eternal knocking. She could hear her mother so clearly. It didn't feel like a memory. It felt like it was happening. Like she was living through it again.

"Are you okay?" Hazel whispered, and Jac nodded, not trusting herself to say anything more.

"Can we try and get out of here, then?" Sam said, stomping down the hall and back to the door they'd found. Hazel and Jac walked side by side, and Jac could feel Hazel's eyes on her, but she did not dare look at him.

When they reached the door, Sam tried the knob again and this time it swung open.

"Weird how these doors only open when you're here," Sam said, looking over his shoulder at Jac.

"What does that mean?" Hazel asked.

"Nothing, let's go," Sam muttered.

The trio looked at each other for a beat, and then first Jac and then Hazel stepped through the door.

Before Sam could join them, someone or some*thing* stopped him.

The last thing he said was, "What the?" Then the screaming started.

Jac and Hazel spun around. Sam was being dragged down the hallway floor on his belly. His feet disappeared into an increasing darkness that threatened to swallow him whole. His arms desperately tried to find purchase on the broken furniture as he was pulled away from them. But no matter how much they yelled, unable to hear themselves over the endless shrieking, he vanished into the dark. Once again, it was silent; then the door slammed shut.

10

"SAM!" HAZEL SCREAMED, YANKING ON THE DOORKNOB, THE FLAT OF his hand banging and banging against the wood. "Sam, can you hear me?"

"What just happened?"

"I don't know! Something got him!" Hazel tugged so hard on the doorknob, Jac was sure it was going to come off in his hand.

"How is the door locked again? It was *just* open!"

"I don't know!" Hazel yelled. He banged the flat of his hand on the door. "Sam! Sam! Are you there?" He laid his head against the wood of the door, and Jac watched his shoulders hitch as he started to cry.

Jac pulled out her phone. "I'll call him. Maybe I can call him."

At this Hazel perked up a little. "You have his number?"

"Yeah, we're lab partners. We had to meet up a few times for projects."

Her hand hovered over Sam's number. She wanted to try it, she really did, but she couldn't stop thinking about what had happened in the parlor when Hazel tried to call for help. She shook her head. No, that didn't matter. Making sure Sam was okay mattered more.

She tapped the number and listened to the phone ring. *Come on, pick up, Sam. Pick up.* Suddenly the ringing stopped and there was a clicking noise, then something that sounded like static.

"Sam?" Jac said gingerly. "Can you hear me?"

"Sam!" Hazel yelled into the phone. "We're on the other side of the door. Knock if you're okay!"

There was a beat and then someone, or some*thing*, answered.

"Sssssaaaaaaaaaaaaaaaaaaaammmmmmmmmm."

The voice was low, deep, and soggy, dragging out the word with a wet popping sound like water was bubbling out of their mouth. It vibrated through her ears and lodged itself in her brain. Jac's hand shook as she held the phone before tapping the End Call button. But it didn't work, and that wet gurgling sound still pulsed through the speaker, calling for Sam. She tried again and again, jamming her finger on the button. Finally the horrible voice cut out and something sparked, like a shock of static that flared bright. With a yelp, Jac dropped her phone. When she picked it back up, the screen was black and hot. With shaking hands, she slipped it back into her pocket.

"Oh, man," Hazel said. "What was that noise?"

"I don't know. But it wasn't Sam."

"Do you . . . think he's dead?" Hazel covered his face, and Jac watched his shoulders start to shake. "We're going to die in here." He said it low, barely a whisper, but each word fell like a stone.

"We're going be okay," she told him. It was one of those things that people said all the time, even though they didn't know if it was going to be okay, or worse, when they definitely knew it wasn't going to be okay. It was the kind of stuff that Jac hated. She overheard her doctor one time and learned the word for this kind of phrase was *platitude*. At the time it made her think of the word *plateau*, a flat, inescapable ground. These were the kind of statements that people made when they didn't know what else to say. When they find themselves on a flat, inescapable ground and they don't realize that sometimes silence is okay too. And here she was now, laying a gentle hand on Hazel's shoulder as he cried, offering up this platitude that they were going to be okay when all signs pointed differently.

Except she meant it.

That was the weirdest part. Even with everything terrible that had happened, even with John and Sam disappearing, even with her face engraved on that key, her name on that wall, and that hospital bed, something inside her told her it was going to be okay. Something told her that being in the House was a challenge of some sort. That it could be beat. But only by finishing.

"The only way out is through, Hazel," she said again.

He lifted his head. "What?"

"That's how we'll get out. We need to go through the House."

"How do you know this? And what about John and Sam?"

"I don't know. I just do. I just know this is what it wants."

A hard laugh came from Hazel. "What it *wants*? You make it sound like this place is alive or something."

Jac opened her mouth to respond, almost unsure of what words were going to come out, but closed it when suddenly lights started to flicker on in the room. The two of them spun around as overhead chandeliers sputtered to life. Candle sconces attached to the walls flared bright, lighting up the space. And it was definitely not a space they expected. It wasn't filthy or creepy at all. In fact it was kind of lovely.

They were in a library.

Floor-to-ceiling bookshelves were stuffed, sometimes even overstuffed, with books. Some were slender, no bigger than her pinkie; some were so wide she'd need both hands and probably some help getting them down. The room was huge and wide, with a wraparound balcony like the one in the parlor. There was also one of those ladders on wheels that you could zip around the room on, pulling books from the highest shelf.

Jac loved libraries and she treasured books, so in many ways this room should have, or at least could have, brought her comfort if it were in any other house. But this library had something more.

It was also filled with desks, not in neat classroom lines but jumbled together carelessly, and on each desk was a typewriter, the old kind that had high black keys that seemed like they would jam all the time. A piece of paper was rolled into each carriage. But this was not the worst part.

The worst part was that every desk was empty and yet every typewriter was typing.

Jac watched the keys go up and down, the carriages slide and ding. She watched the papers start to fill with words from the invisible hands that were typing. The cacophony of clacking keys. She shuddered. How were these typewriters moving on their own?

"What is happening?" Hazel whispered.

"I don't know," Jac said, not taking her eyes off the nearest typewriter as the keys went up and down, up and down, and the words appeared dark and inky on the white paper.

"It has to be a trick," Hazel said. "Some sort of automated thing."

Jac nodded, but in her heart she did not agree.

Hazel's eyes went wide. "OF COURSE!" he shouted. "Yes, that's it! It's all a trick. This is a prank. In fact, I bet Sam and John set this up. They're the ones who are doing all of this. I'm sure of it. I mean, think about it. First off, they're the ones that disappeared, which means they could be anywhere. Secondly, Sam accused us of playing a trick on them, and that feels like a classic way to throw us off the trail that it's really them! I can't believe they thought they could fool us." As he spoke, his voice was getting louder and louder as it all came together for him. Then, at the top of his lungs, he yelled, "YOU'RE NOT SCARING ME, JOHN! YOU HEAR ME, SAM? I'M NOT FALL-ING FOR THIS!"

Jac squeezed his arm. "Hazel, stop."

"What?"

"Look," she whispered. "Listen."

The keys had stopped. No more clacking, no more clicking. No more noise like little teeth chattering. Instead, the room was quiet. Horribly, terribly quiet.

"The only way out is through," she said to Hazel. When he didn't answer, she said, "You hear me?"

He turned a nervous face toward her and managed a hard swallow and a nod. "You really don't think it's John and Sam?"

"I really don't, Hazel. I'm sorry. I know you want that, but I don't know. I just know we have to try and get out. Safely."

Hazel glanced around the too quiet, too still library. "What do we do? We need to get help."

Jac swallowed hard and then softly said, "There is no getting help, okay? It might be easier for you if you stop thinking about this place like that."

"What do you mean?"

"It's just . . . I think there are rules here. But they're not the same rules as out there. There is only you and me and getting through this." She nodded her head toward a door at the back of the library.

Hazel saw it for the first time, and his shoulders lifted. He nodded his head and swallowed hard. "Okay," he said.

Jac took a tentative step forward toward the first row of typewriters, and Hazel followed reluctantly. As soon as they moved, the keys on the typewriters started again, clacking and clicking like chattering teeth, an image she couldn't get out of her head. The desks were close together in many places and not in straight lines, so that instead of walking easily down the rows they had to weave their way around. She stepped lightly, carefully, between the desks, anxious about accidentally touching them, twisting her body so that she cleared the narrow spaces without disturbing anything. She glanced down at a paper on one typewriter's carriage and saw the words *my death*.

A terrible thought spread through her like a cold flush. It filled her chest first and then her lungs until she felt like she couldn't breathe. What if the typewriters weren't working on their own? What if Hazel was wrong and it wasn't a trick?

What if they were haunted?

What if each seat was filled with the invisible body of someone who hadn't found their way out? Someone who didn't survive the House. Each seat could be filled with a ghost, stuck here telling the story of their death. Or worse, Jac realized as she peeked another look at another slip of paper. Yes, some were telling the story of their death, but others just the fleeting and few memories about their lives? She shuddered, unable to stop herself.

Keep going, she told herself. *The only way out is through.*

"Why are you stopping?" Hazel whispered behind her.

Jac cleared her throat but said nothing. There was no point in panicking him further. She stepped carefully between the next set of desks.

But if there were ghosts clacking away at their typewriters, they seemed to ignore her. The noise filled the library, punctuated occasionally by the ding of the carriage reaching the end of the row and the zip as it returned. As they moved through the room, Jac was unable to stop herself from glancing down at each paper. Some were in languages she didn't know. Those that were in English had sentences that startled her.

We are only bones until that too is gone. Then we are nothing. Nothing but haunted memories in the House.

She glanced back at Hazel behind her, but he ignored the papers. His eyes were focused on the door ahead of them. She glanced down at another page.

Life is rare and fleeting, and when it is gone there is nothing anyone can do about it.

If she didn't find her way out, was this what would happen to her? To Hazel? Would they just be ghosts trapped here forever, reliving the worst parts of their death? Missing their family and their friends? Missing life? She shuddered again but moved on.

In the center of the room, she passed another desk. There was a typewriter on it, a sheet of paper curled around the roller just like the others. But no one was typing on this one. The words were already written, and they caught Jac's eye. They were words she recognized.

Symptoms include: headaches, nausea, speech or balance issues, difficulty swallowing, weakness or numbness in arms and legs, double vision.

Tumor—Malignant
Prognosis—Poor
Malignant
Poor
Malignant

Jac reached down with shaking hands and pulled the paper from the roller. The words *malignant* and *poor* filled the page. Her vision swam as she read the words over again. It was suddenly hard to swallow, and her hands and feet started to tingle. She felt her breath hitch and then hitch again.

She knew these words, had learned them and the horror they caused at far too young an age.

"What is that?" Hazel asked, trying to see the paper. "What does it say?"

No. She couldn't tell Hazel. She couldn't tell anyone. Not ever. If she said it out loud, it would come true. It would all happen again, and she would be strapped to that conveyor belt that went in only one direction and ended in only one place. That's what those two words together meant.

They meant death.

No, she thought. *Don't even think it.*

First, she balled up the piece of paper and then, changing her mind, she started to tear it up. The urge to destroy it, to make it disappear, was overwhelming. Her hands shook as she worked, ripping the sheet apart into the tiniest portions so that no part was bigger than her fingernail, her breath coming in ragged gasps. *Make it disappear. Make it disappear.*

"What are you doing?" Hazel whispered, but she ignored him. "Come on, we have to go."

He moved past her, making his way toward the door, leaving her standing over that typewriter.

This is not my future, she decided. She was going to

the be the one who made it. She was going to survive. She looked down at the carnage at her feet, at the litter of torn scraps of paper that lay on her sneakers and the floor.

She felt a power she hadn't in a while. As if by destroying the words she was destroying her past, changing the whole timeline, deleting the pain, and then also—and most important—altering her future.

Which could then be the same as destroying the return of it all, which she was sure waited for her somewhere down the road. Tearing up the words meant no doctor would ever look at her again with that sad look. Would never say out loud the thing she and her mother feared the most.

It's over because I say it's over. Yes, Jac felt a power she had never known. As if her future was now as unmarked as everyone else's. She didn't have to carry those words around with her. But that feeling, as needed as it was, sadly did not last.

Because as she stood there, staring down at the torn pieces of paper, Jac watched in horror as they started to slide together, started to knit themselves back into a whole, the fibers of the paper reaching out like fingers and fusing together, the ink, like dripping paint, now re-creating those words she'd tried so hard to ignore.

Jac kicked at them, trying to spread them apart, trying somehow to make it untrue. Something inside her head started to pound. A knocking. Knocking. Knocking. And then the hard, startling blast of the air horn. She flinched and Hazel stared at her, wide-eyed, but already he seemed so far away.

No, Jac thought, and then squeezed her eyes shut. *Calm down. You're not in the Machine. It's not happening. It's just the House.* She took a deep breath and then another, willing her heart to stop rattling inside her. She laid her hand over it and listened to its steady strong beat, letting it center her, calm her.

You're alive, she reminded herself. She had lived. Whatever that paper said didn't change the fact that she was alive.

For now, a voice that did not sound like her own whispered silkily in her ear, and she spun around to see if someone was behind her, but she was alone.

She looked down at the typewriter. That terrible paper with its terrible truths was back snug inside the typewriter carriage, taunting her like a terrible dream you remember in the morning. It sat there, those dark, inked words staring up at her, challenging her. Letting her know they would not just disappear. That she must at some point face them.

Jac's hands started to shake again. She reached

down and with a cry yanked the page out of the roller and proceeded to tear it up all over again. While she was doing so, she was vaguely aware of someone screaming and she wondered, briefly, if it was her.

When that paper was again torn to bits and fluttered to her feet, Jac looked around the room. With a slow sick horror, she realized that both the knocking and the sound of clicking typewriter keys had stopped. The silence seemed deafening. Though she couldn't see them, she could *feel* the ghosts watching her. As she glanced around the room, she swore she could catch a snippet, something you could see only when you looked away. A pale face. The wisp of a hand. Hollow black eyes. A shrouded figure.

Then like Frankenstein's monster stuttering to life, the ghosts, previously invisible, started to materialize right in front of her. They flickered and faded and then grew stronger until Jac could see nearly all of them. They sat at their desks—long-fingered hands curled over the typewriters but not typing. Instead, each ghostly head turned toward Jac, locked on her with eyes hollow and black. Their hair was ragged and wet; water ran down their faces from some invisible source, dripped off their fingers, splashing onto the keys of the typewriters. It pooled at their feet. Their empty eyes were just black sockets, and a green hue seemed to shine off their skin. Jac started to shake a little looking at them as they stared at her, ragged and wet, hair hanging in clumps, faces gaunt, lips blackened and dead. The smell was awful.

Jac's breath hitched. She had to get out of here. She heard Hazel yell her name. He was at the other door and waving for her to join him.

"Come on, Jac! What are you waiting for?"

As soon as he spoke, the ghosts then turned to look at him. But their attention barely lingered on Hazel in the doorway, waving for her to hurry up. The ghosts had already swiveled back to Jac, standing in front of the desk that she now worried belonged to her.

No. I'm not one of you. I'm not one of the dead.

Then there was a voice inside her. A wet, dark voice, a voice that dripped water, that filled her mouth and nose and brain with a foul sewer smell, a voice that echoed up from her belly, filling her throat, said, *But aren't you? Are you sure?*

And as if to answer that question, the ghosts rose out of their chairs and hovered in the air above their desks for a split second, their dark, hollow eyes, their stretched faces, turned toward her. It was long enough for Jac to realize that now she must run.

They were on her quick, howling in her ear, desperate to tell their stories. She heard snatches of them as she pushed desks over, typewriters clanging loudly to the floor. She vaulted over a few chairs as she ran as fast as she could toward Hazel. But the ghosts were everywhere, their faces looming up in front of her, a hiss on their lips, a snarl buried deep in their throats. They caught at her clothing and pulled on her hair. Jac batted at them, but her hand passed through. Only the ghosts seemed able to hang on to her. She tried to shake them off.

Take us with you, living girl.

Free us from the House.

Or stay.

Stay forever.

This is where you belong. You are one of us now.

Jac could feel their anger, their bitterness, and their hatred. She was alive and they were not, and they were determined to keep her here. She shook her head and batted at them, still pushing over chairs and squeezing past desks. *Don't listen to them*, she told herself. *You're alive. You're alive.*

A voice rumbled through the walls and floorboards. A voice louder than any of the ghosts, louder than Jac's own thoughts, and without knowing how she knew she realized it was the House.

But are you? Are you, Jacqueline Price-Dupree, actually alive?

11

HER LUNGS BURNED. GHOST HANDS WERE STILL CATCHING AT HER face, tugging at her hair. She could feel them, cold and wet, gripping at her shoulders and arms, trying to pull her back to them. Their faces appearing and then disappearing in front of her as she ducked and dodged them; hissing, snarling voices begging her to take them with her. To save them from the House. To free them.

Frantic to get away from them, Jac raced forward, pushing desks out of her way until she finally reached Hazel. He had one hand outstretched, the other gripping the doorway. He grabbed her hand and yanked her through the door and then kicked it shut behind him. The ghosts pulled on the handle from the other side, rattling and shaking it, demanding to be saved. Jac lay on the floor panting, her heart flipping over just as fast as her stomach. She could still smell them, that dank, dirty water smell. For a brief second, she thought she might throw up. She gagged once and then again.

"Are you okay?" Hazel asked.

But she couldn't talk. She could barely breathe. She squeezed her eyes shut, but all she saw were those dark letters typed on that page. It was painted on her brain now. *Malignant tumor with a poor prognosis.* But how did the House know? She had never told anyone. Not even Hazel. Only she and her mother knew what had happened. About the surgeries and the tests and the radiation. About the way the doctor sat her mother down and in no uncertain terms offered grim news.

Malignant tumor with a poor prognosis. Those words were permanent, and there was no way she could tear it up. There was no way to forget. The House knew, and it cruelly wanted her to know it knew. There were no secrets here. There was no hiding.

Hazel reached down and put a hand on her shoulder. "Jac?"

She jumped at his touch and scooted backward away from him.

"Jac, it's just me. It's Hazel."

"Did they get through?" she asked. Her eyes, unable to focus on anything, darted around the room searching for their wet faces.

"Who?"

Jac hesitated at first but then, no longer caring how it sounded, said, "The ghosts?"

"What ghosts? What are you talking about?"

"You couldn't see them?" Jac asked, squeezing her eyes shut. Was this another symptom? Another hallucination? She felt like she was slipping, and in that fear and unease, she felt the House sigh and settle. Was it satisfied? Is this what it wanted? To break her?

Jac looked down at her hands, which trembled slightly. *That's just fear. That's not a tremor. That's not a symptom. That was my past. It doesn't mean it's my future.*

It was something her mother said often, a hand laid on her back as she pushed Jac higher on the swings, the breeze warm and sweet in her hair. This was two years after everything was done. "That was your past, sweetie. It doesn't mean it is your future. You get what everybody gets."

She never had the nerve to ask what that meant. What did everybody get? What was the promise? What was the guarantee? Jac wasn't sure she wanted to know.

She took a deep breath and tried to swallow but found that her mouth was too dry. "They were sitting at the typewriters."

"Jac, the seats at the typewriters were empty." Hazel hesitated and then met her gaze. "I didn't see any ghosts."

"They were there. They were telling their stories, about their lives and . . . deaths. They were typing them out, and then they saw me and they just came after me."

"I . . . didn't see anything," Hazel said. "I mean, I saw you, with that paper. You looked scared and then you just started running like . . . something was chasing you."

"You believe me though, right?" Jac looked up at him, wiping the tears from her cheeks. "Please, you have to believe me."

"I believe you, Jac." Hazel sat down and put an arm around her shoulder. It was a kind gesture, and right now, trapped inside this cursed House, she was so thankful for his presence, she could have wept.

"Can I ask you a question? The paper you tore up . . . what did it say?" Hazel asked.

"It was . . . for me. It was . . . mine."

"Your what?"

"My story."

"What did it say?" Hazel asked, his eyes wide and frightened.

But Jac couldn't answer that. She couldn't make her mouth form those words, because they were so much more than just words. They were dark, deep nightmares. They were the sound of her mother crying in the night when she thought Jac was fast asleep. They were the sound of the air horn and the knocking. They were doctors that got her name wrong and whose breath always smelled like coffee.

They were a death sentence.

Instead she said, "The ghosts, they noticed me. They made themselves visible. They . . . tried to keep me there."

Hazel furrowed his brow. "That's horrible. That's . . . oh, that just makes my stomach hurt. They aren't here now, right? They didn't get through, did they?"

"No," Jac said, her eyes darting around the room, searching for blackened lips, wet hair, gauzy green skin. "No, it's just us."

"What did they look like?" Hazel asked.

Jac closed her eyes and shook her head slowly.

"On second thought I don't want to know," Hazel said quickly. "Don't tell me."

Suddenly the doorknob to the library started to

turn slowly. Jac and Hazel both watched it, neither of them breathing. It turned to the left, creaking.

"Jac," Hazel whispered, but she shushed him just as quickly.

Then the knob started to creak to the right. Slowly. Slowly. There was a brief pause when Hazel and Jac held their breath, when nothing happened, when the doorknob lay still and silent and Jac believed they were safe before it started to rattle in its frame. Hard.

As if someone—or something—on the other side was determined to get out.

With a slight yelp, they both jumped backward, away from the door. They waited a beat and then another, but the door was silent.

"Jac . . . ," Hazel started, lost his nerve, and then started again. "What . . . what was on that paper? What did it say?"

She looked up at him, her vision swimming. His face shifting in and out of focus. Double vision. Just like it said on the paper. Jac shook the thoughts out of her head and looked at her friend. "What?"

"The paper. The one you pulled out of the type-writer. What did it say? Why did you tear it up? You said it was your story. What does that mean?"

Jac squeezed her eyes shut and shook her head. When she opened them again, Hazel was back in focus.

The headache that was squeezing the back of her head throbbed once, then twice, then relented. The relief from the pain was palpable. As if she'd managed to get herself free from the mouth of something ferocious. Something with teeth that would never really let her go. When she was little, she'd had nightmares of a monster that would chase her. A giant shaggy thing, eyes like lamps that shone in every crack so there was no place to hide. A jaw with a tangle of teeth. She knew if it caught her it would eat her up and she would disappear.

"What was it?" Hazel pressed again.

Jac shook her head.

"You can tell me, Jac. You can tell me anything. You know that. We're best friends. That's what best friends do. They trust each other. They keep promises. Maybe . . . "

Hazel gave her a look as he chose his words, and Jac held his gaze, never blinking, like an animal caught in the headlights. "Maybe it will help us. In here. Maybe . . . if I knew why the key was shaped like you, why your name was on the wall, and that paper . . . maybe we can figure it out together. Like best friends do." He let out a small, nervous laugh. "Like two best friends stuck in a crazy story that you root for. Like in a book or something."

Jac looked at her friend. Hazel was only person in school who talked to her, really. The only person it seemed at times that could even see her. When she wasn't with Hazel, she felt like a ghost at school.

But he did something else for her.

He let her forget, even if for the briefest moments, the monster she was running from. A thing with teeth, with lamplight eyes, that chased her. But if she told Hazel now, it would bring the monster to life. She would reveal where she had been hiding, and the monster, with his terrible eyes and terrible dank breath, would find her again. And then Hazel would know. And every time he looked at her, he would see her past. Eventually it would be all he could see. Her illness would be what defined her. And the real Jac would fall into it—like sinking underwater—and her illness would be everything.

It would be all she ever was.

She couldn't let that happen. She needed Hazel to see her as real, as something more than what she'd gone through. If he ever looked at her and that was all he saw, she would break. This was something Jac couldn't bear. With him, she could hide it.

So instead she set her face and met his eyes, and with a voice that sounded darker and deeper and more monstrous than her own, she said, "Please don't ever ask me that, Hazel. Ever."

"But . . . Jac. What if it would help?"

"No. Just don't." She held up a hand. "If you care at all . . . you'll never ask me that question."

"I . . . " But Hazel stopped when he saw the look on her face. Jac could see he was hurt, but she had no choice. She had to keep this one thing. She had to keep Hazel. "Okay, I'm sorry. I just wanted you to know I was here. For anything."

"I know," Jac said, her voice just above a whisper. "Someday, Haze. When I'm ready. I just . . . " Her voice caught. She swallowed hard and tried again. "I just can't right now. Not here. Especially not here."

Not in this House that seemed to know already and mock her for it.

"Okay," Hazel said, nodding, and Jac knew from his face that it was sincere. He was okay with giving her space. It was like the opposite of her mother. Her mother was always hovering. There for every stutter or trip. It was an exhausting way to live. She felt like she was under a microscope. All she wanted was to stop being afraid, but her mother was always worrying and questioning everything. It was sometimes like Jac was the mother, and that made her angry. And that anger bubbled up inside her, fueling her. It was too much to ask of any twelve-year-old. Sometimes Jac just wanted to scream that she was just a kid. Why couldn't she just be a kid?

Jac squeezed her eyes shut.

"You okay?" Hazel asked, interrupting her thoughts. She swiped at the tears and then nodded. Now was not the time for this. Now was the time to focus. If the House was trying to show her something about her past, she could figure it out on her own. She didn't need Hazel to be involved. She would save both of them. She would be the hero.

"The only way out is through," she whispered.

As if in response, the doorknob creaked. Jac and Hazel exchanged a look. Jac was about to suggest they get out of there, when the latch disengaged. The door creaked slowly and terribly open.

Her heart hammering in her ears, she waited for the ghosts—the long, ragged hair, the bubbling mouths, the gray-green skin—to come flying out.

But they didn't. Though Jac was partially right.

The thing crawling through the door definitely had gray skin.

12

FROM THE DARK, YAWNING MAW OF THE DOORWAY STRETCHED TWO gray fingers. They wrapped, wet and sickly long, around the wood of the door, which creaked under their pressure. The two fingers were followed by three more and then another hand, this one with black and broken fingernails.

All the blood seemed to have drained out of Jac's body.

She couldn't move. She couldn't scream. She couldn't even think as she watched whatever had taken John and Sam now finally came for them.

Hazel, thankfully, felt differently. He leaped to his feet, hoisted Jac up. She watched, paralyzed, as a skull, topped with a mane of long, raggedy black hair, started to appear around the door. Whatever it was, it wore some sort of veil over its face. Its eyes were obscured, just two dark smears, and its mouth opened then like a black hole.

And that was when the screaming started.

It was the same wailing that they'd heard in the House earlier, the same wailing that had come out of Hazel's phone.

Finally Jac could move again, with Hazel tugging her on. And they ran, arms and legs pumping, straight down the endless hallway. And the woman, the creature, whatever it was, chased them. Jac could feel it just behind her, gray fingers outstretched, wanting to grab her, catch her, and pull her into the walls of this House and make her a ghost herself. And the shrieking was horrible. It filled her ears but also her mouth and lungs until Jac couldn't be sure she wasn't the one doing all the screaming.

Jac and Hazel pushed harder, but it didn't matter. That thing—whatever it was—was faster. It gained on them. Even though Jac knew she shouldn't, she couldn't help herself and turned for a quick glance over her shoulder. Her stomach dropped, and she immediately wished she hadn't done that. Because the creature that was chasing them was not running like them, on its own two legs. Instead it was scurrying on all fours, like an insect, its arms and legs bent at impossible angles, its head still horribly upright, those dark eyes watching, that mouth always open, always screaming.

The hallway stretched before them, doorways filled both sides, but Jac was so afraid if she stopped running then the thing behind her would catch her. Finally, Hazel glanced over his shoulder, saw what Jac must have seen, made a horrified noise, and sped up. He grabbed the next door on the left, yanked it open, and both he and Jac dived through it. They hit the floor hard. The door slammed shut behind them, finally and mercifully cutting off the shrieking.

Panting and terrified, they looked up to find themselves in the parlor again. Hazel and Jac both sprang up and threw themselves at the door, to stop whatever it was that was chasing them from getting in.

But the hall was quiet, as was this room, minus their panting breaths.

That is, it was quiet until it wasn't.

Until a voice behind them spoke. "The Offer Has Been Accepted."

Jac and Hazel spun around, and in front of them was an impossibly tall, impossibly thin man. In fact, he towered over them, and Jac reasoned he had to be nine feet tall even though it seemed impossible that anyone could be so tall. And so slender, his limbs almost freakishly long, as if he were nothing but bone under his clothes. He wore a rich black cloak, as dark as deep space, and a mask with a long, hooked beak like a bird's. For a moment the image of the woman who ran the Machine flashed through Jac's brain and then dissolved. Without knowing how, Jac knew he was the owner of this House.

He removed his mask to reveal a pale visage that should have terrified them. For the man before her, if he was even a man, had no eyes. No nose. No ears. He was nothing but the razor-thin crisscrossing of scar tissue. Except for his mouth. He had a large, wide jaw like that of a serpent. Jac had never felt more seen than she did by this strange creature before her. Even if he had no eyes. When he spoke, it was softly but firmly, as if he had never been questioned about anything he said. She felt his voice all the way down to her bones.

"The Offer Has Been Accepted. The Challenge Has Begun. The House Is Yours."

"W-what does that mean?" Hazel whispered.

"What is this place?" Jac asked. Part of her brain knew she should be terrified, and part of her was. But the rest of her needed answers.

"It is many things. It is a House. It is a story. It is a confession. It exists in this time and space to serve you. You have called for it, and it has come for you. The Challenge Has Begun."

"Where are Sam and John?" Hazel asked.

But the man before them continued to direct his comments only at Jac. As if Hazel weren't even there.

"I don't know what the challenge is," Jac said, trying to keep her voice steady. "I didn't ask for anything."

"You did. You called the House into existence, and it came. Now you must leave something behind."

"What?" Jac asked.

"Everyone leaves something different in the House. A memory. A feeling. But most of all a truth. Your truth."

"My truth about what?"

"That is for the House to decide. That is the pact."

"Who are you?"

"I am Mr. Nobody. I care for the House and all who still walk its halls." He paused here, tilting his head to the side as if he could hear something through his nothing ears. Hazel and Jac exchanged a look, but Mr. Nobody continued, "You have the key. Find your cabinet. Before the Mourner finds you."

At the sound of the word *Mourner*, a scream

sprouted from behind the door. Hazel scrambled to the door they'd come through and threw his shoulder against it should anything try to scuttle out.

But the cry died down, and when it did, they found themselves strangely alone. Mr. Nobody was gone, vanished like one of the library ghosts.

"The Challenge Has Begun," Jac whispered, repeating his cryptic words. "The Offer Has Been Accepted."

It felt as if the entire House settled just now, as if in a sigh. Though she could not be sure if it was a sigh of relief or not. Hazel looked at Jac and then at the empty parlor Mr. Nobody had left behind. "I want to get out of here."

"I know," Jac said even as her hand floated down to her pocket and ever so lightly touched the key.

"What did he mean about this key and the cabinet?" Hazel asked.

"I don't know," Jac whispered. But inside something stirred. The Mourner. That was the name that Mr. Nobody had used. And Jac could not pretend it was not familiar. It was a name she had, when she was younger, attached to a particular nightmare. A woman who screamed. A woman who chased.

"The Mourner, of course," she whispered.

"What are you talking about? Who is the Mourner?"

"The woman who screams. The one who took John and Sam."

"The creature we just ran from? How could you possibly know her name?"

And in that moment, Jac came the closest she'd ever come to telling Hazel the truth. All of it. The fact that her nightmares, real and imagined, had all somehow found their way into this House. It was right there, all the words clawing their way up her throat and banging against her teeth, desperate to come out. Because what a relief it would be.

To finally tell the truth.

Your truth, the House whispered softly in her ear. *You must leave behind your truth.*

Jac shivered at the voice in her head that was not her own but was still somehow a deeply and strangely familiar voice.

"Jac," Hazel said, pulling her out of her thoughts. "What is going on?"

"I'm not sure," she said, realizing that she couldn't tell Hazel. Not now. Maybe not ever. "This has to be the key he was talking about." She pulled the key from her pocket, and Hazel took it and looked it over.

"It really does look like you."

"I know."

"And the writing on the wall back there. About

this being the house you were entering always. What does that mean?"

"I don't know. Mr. Nobody said we had to find my cabinet before the Mourner finds us."

Hazel shuddered. "And the Mourner is that . . . screaming creature."

"I think so." It was somewhere between the truth and a lie. She knew that creature was the Mourner because the House had plucked her directly out of Jac's head. But saying that seemed impossible. How could she explain to Hazel that the House knew her? That it knew what happened and it knew what she feared the most. It sounded absurd.

"Okay, so let's find your cabinet," Hazel said, and reached for the nearest door. He pulled on the handle, but it was locked. He tried the next. It was also locked. "Okay, one of them has to be open, right? That's the way it's been this whole time."

She watched him go from door to door, cursing and yelling that this was impossible. Hazel climbed the balcony steps and tried each door up there.

Frustrated and scared, he started kicking one of them. He slammed his hand against the wood and screamed, "Let us out!"

"Haze," Jac said softly. "Come back down here."

Hazel trudged across the balcony and down the

stairs, slumping down on the last one. "We're trapped."

"We're not trapped. We just haven't found a way out yet. They're not the same thing," Jac said, looking at the key. "This key is the way out. I know it is."

"Through which door? I tried them all."

Had they tried all the doors? She glanced around the room, up at the balcony. Hazel had tried each door up there, and each one was locked. The House was keeping them in this room. And if that was the case, there had to be a reason. This whole time the doors had opened when the House wanted them to open and closed when it was showing her something. So what was it showing her now?

Jac started walking around the room. Every few steps she knocked the heel of her sneaker hard on the ground, as if testing the wood, listening for that hollow sound that indicated there was something else, some kind of space or cubby. When she reached the carpet in the center of the room, she stopped.

"Help me with this," she said. Hazel got up, and they each grabbed an end of the heavy rug and pulled it to the side. On the floor, previously hidden by the rug, was a trapdoor. Jac reached for the latch.

"Wait," Hazel said. "We don't know where that leads."

"I know, but we do know that all the other doors

lead right back in. We have to try something else, Hazel. The only way out is through, right?"

She paused, her hand clutching the latch. Hazel put his on it too, and they exchanged a look and he nodded, almost imperceptibly.

"On the count of three," he said.

"Wait."

"What?"

"I'm sorry, Hazel. I shouldn't have ever come inside this House."

Hazel held her gaze and said, "We all came in." He gave her a look that let something important pass between them—something neither of them could really say. Something that meant it was somehow going to be okay even if nothing felt okay. "Count of three."

Jac nodded. And together they said, "One, two, three."

They pulled hard and the trapdoor swung upward.

13

THEY STARED DOWN THE HOLE. THERE WAS NOTHING BUT A LADDER disappearing into the darkness below them with no end in sight.

"Nope," Hazel said, sitting back on his butt. "There is no way we're going down there."

"What if it's the only way out?"

"We don't know that. What if we climb down that ladder and come right through the ceiling into here?"

"Then we'll know where it leads."

"Jac, stop. This is ridiculous."

"Haze, what other choice do we have? None of these other doors lead anywhere. We can either try this or spend the rest of our lives in this parlor. We certainly can't call for help. I, for one, don't feel like starving to death here hoping that someone is going to find us. Also, she's out there somewhere." Jac got up and found a nearby candle that was burning on one of the end tables. She picked it up and carried it back over to the ladder.

"She could be down there too," Hazel said.

"Okay, but what if it leads to my cabinet and then we can get out of here even quicker?"

"You're just going to go down there?" Hazel asked. "You're just going to climb down this dark, creepy hole in the floor in this twisted house like it's no big deal?"

"What choice do we have? Look, I came in here. I dared John 'cause I thought I could handle this. I was wrong. But I still did this."

"Jac . . . "

"And I'm going to get us back out. That's all that matters."

"By finding your cabinet?"

"That's what Mr. Nobody said. We have to find it before the Mourner does."

"I hate all of this," Hazel said, getting up off the floor and grabbing his own candle from the end table.

"Me too." Jac gripped the candle with one hand and the ladder with the other.

"Wait, maybe I should go first," Hazel said.

"Why?"

"Because I'm . . . a dude. Make sure it's safe."

Jac snorted and laughed. Even if his logic was totally off, even when he was completely wrong, at least he tried. If nothing else, he definitely tried. "Okay, whatever, Haze."

She proceeded to climb down the ladder first, carefully gripping the candle so that it didn't fall but also carefully gripping the rungs so that she, too, didn't fall. Hazel stayed a few rungs above her. As they passed down through the floor the air got colder, as if they were entering a basement.

Suddenly a loud bang came from above. Jac gripped the ladder even tighter, her heart thudding in her chest. Hazel whimpered. They both looked up and saw that the trapdoor had closed.

Or worse, had been shut.

"It probably just fell," Hazel said with a thin, uncertain voice.

"Probably," Jac echoed. "Ready?"

"No," Hazel said as they continued down the ladder. With the door shut, the light from the candle provided small comfort, but Jac also knew that if she didn't have it her eyes would adjust to the dark that much quicker. Now all she could see was whatever that small circle of light allowed. And that wasn't very much.

"Any end in sight?" Hazel whispered above her. Jac stopped, held her candle out to see if she could spot the ground, but all she saw were more ladder rungs stretching into darkness.

"Not that I can see."

"This is some Alice in Wonderland nonsense right here," Hazel muttered above her, and Jac couldn't help but smile, even as her fear made her hands and her grip slippery.

"Could be worse. Alice fell."

"Why'd you have to say that?" Hazel moaned.

They continued to descend, rung after rung into the darkness. Jac reasoned they had to be a hundred feet underground at this point. How much farther could they go? When her feet finally hit the soft dirt ground below her, she practically wept. At least she was off the ladder. Her arms were shaking from holding on so tight. She glanced up to see Hazel.

"Just a few more rungs and you're on the ground," she told him.

Once he was off the ladder, he held his candle up so they could get a view of their new surroundings. The walls were stone bricks, the floor was soft dirt, and the room wrapped around them in a circle. The whole thing couldn't have been more than twenty feet wide. It was a stone dungeon, a well of some sort. There had to be a way out somewhere.

"We just have to find the door," Jac said, feeling along the walls.

"There is no door," a voice behind them said. Out of the darkness a terrifying face loomed. It was pale, hairless, the nose just two holes in its skin, its eyes wide and white, pupils dilated to such an extreme size that the whole of the iris seemed black. It had a wide terrible mouth with jagged teeth. They were looking upon a face that had not seen light in a very long time. The worst part was the smell of rotting meat that hung around it. "You can't get back out."

"Who are you?" Jac asked, her voice just above a whisper.

"We are the Keeper."

"Keeper? Of what?"

"What did you mean we can't get out?" Hazel said, holding up his candle. "The ladder is right . . . " But he trailed off as he stared into the emptiness. Jac felt her breath hitch when she realized the ladder was gone. One moment it had been there, and the next it vanished. They were trapped. Again. *This can't be happening.*

"Where are we?" Jac asked, trying to keep the logical part of her brain in the driver's seat.

135

"The Oubliette."

"What is an oubliette?"

"The Forgetting Room. It's where the House puts you to forget about you."

Jac and Hazel exchanged a look over their candles before Hazel turned toward the wall, frantically looking for an exit. He kept circling around Jac and the Keeper until she started to feel dizzy. "Hazel, stop."

"There's no door. There's no door or a ladder," Hazel said through ragged breath.

"Hazel, calm down."

"We're trapped, Jac. We were safer up in the parlor. We're never going to get out."

"Yes, we are."

"There's no door! We're trapped! We're going to die!"

"*Hazel!* Just stop," Jac yelled. She didn't mean to. She didn't like yelling, not when she did it (and certainly not when other people did), but she could tell Hazel was full of adrenaline and that was making him panic. Sometimes a loud voice is the only thing adrenaline will listen to.

"How do we get out?" she said to the Keeper.

"Oh, we are very smart. We think we know the House, do we? We think we have this all figured out?"

"I know there must be a way to move on."

"From the Forgetting Room?" The Keeper laughed now with a ragged wheeze. "What if we have been forgotten?"

"It doesn't make any sense for us to be forgotten. Why would the House call us here, bait us, just to lock us away?"

"The House did not call you. You called it. Silly girl, thinking she knows how the House works. How it thinks. If it cares."

"Tell me how we get out. Where is the door?"

The Keeper pointed at her. "Stupid girl."

Jac paused to think. Clearly asking about doors didn't seem to work. If their passage was going to come from another way, the question of how they were going to get out wasn't the right question. If it was like a game, she needed to find her way to the next chess space. "Okay. How do we move on?"

The Keeper smiled, a gruesome smile, its jagged teeth jutting from its wide-open mouth. "Riddles."

Jac took a deep breath. She could do this. She knew she could. She was smart. So was Hazel. "What's the riddle?"

Next to her Hazel was starting to calm down, now that he saw there was some slim possible hope that they were going to live.

"If you answer correctly, I will show you the way.

Incorrectly, you will give me yours."

"My what?"

The Keeper stretched out its pale arms and opened its clawlike hands. In them were a number of keys just like the one that Jac had. All those faces. All those other people.

So those were the stakes? If she answered correctly, they would move on. If she didn't, she would be trapped in the House forever. Would it make them ghosts? Or something worse? A nightmare like the Mourner? Hazel stood at her side, staring down at the keys in the creature's hands. Though he had calmed down a bit, his cheeks were still tearstained and his fear wicked off him like so much heat.

"What is the riddle?" he asked.

The Keeper smiled that same mocking grin and said,

> *"What the wealthy crave and the unfortunate have*
> *galore,*
> *is also what the most contented person hungers for.*
> *It is the thing one fears more than death or strife,*
> *but also needs more than life.*
> *What the hoarder loses and the waster saves,*
> *and the only thing we take to our graves."*

A beat passed, and both Jac and Hazel exhaled. Jac closed her eyes and repeated the riddle to herself. She could do this. She knew she could. Riddles were always more obvious than people thought. That's how you got tripped up—looking for the harder answer when the right one is in front of you.

"Okay, let's do this," Hazel said, with surprising optimism. "What do the rich want that poor people have?"

Jac shook her head. "What does one fear more than death?"

"I don't know. I don't think there's anything that people fear more than death."

"There has to be something. Pain? Rejection?"

"Being trapped in an Oubliette?" Hazel dryly offered.

A laugh came out of the Keeper. Jac ignored it. *Think. Think.*

"This doesn't make any sense," Hazel said. "We can't do this."

"You can't give up. Come on, we've just started. What do contented people hunger for?"

"I don't know," Hazel said, his voice going high. "If you're happy you don't want anything, right? Isn't that the point of life? This riddle is nonsense."

Jac heard it then. A creaking sound. They both craned their necks and looked upward. A shaft of light shone down on the Oubliette.

The trapdoor had been opened.

There was a low keening cry then. A wail that

threatened to bring the stones of the Oubliette down. The sound vibrated right through Jac's bones. *No. Not now. Not yet.*

Next to her she heard Hazel whimper.

"She is coming for you," the Keeper said. "Better hurry now. Better guess. Only one guess though. Better be right."

As the woman's cries echoed down the shaft, Jac watched as she started to appear at the mouth of the Oubliette, scaling down the brick walls like a spider. She crawled, skittered, seemingly immune to gravity, down the long shaft of the tunnel, her arms bent at strange angles like an insect's, her hands finding seemingly impossible holds between the bricks of the Oubliette. It was as if gravity didn't exist, and it was unnerving to watch. Just as unnerving as the cries still pummeling them from above. Jac and Hazel dropped their candles to cover their ears. They were running out of time. She needed to solve the riddle right now.

"What do people fear more than death but need more than life?" she yelled over the cries of the Mourner.

"It's a trick! There's nothing that anyone loves more than life or fears more than death," Hazel yelled. "Nothing! Absolutely nothing! None of this makes any sense!"

Absolutely nothing.

Nothing. And then it all made wonderful, perfect sense to Jac. There was nothing people loved more than life or feared more than death. There was nothing that the poor had that rich would need. A contented person requires nothing. The hoarder spends nothing, and the waster saves nothing. And it is nothing that everyone carried to their graves!

"Of course!" Jac said. "You're brilliant, Hazel. Absolutely brilliant."

She spun toward the Keeper. "It's nothing. The answer to your riddle is nothing."

The Keeper smiled. "Clever. You might live through this after all," it said, before knocking on the stone walls. "Must be quick." It pointed back up at the Mourner, who was just a few feet above them now, her veil hanging down like a shroud. Behind it Jac could see the faint outline of a mouth opened in that unstoppable shriek. She could leap down from where she was, and they would be cornered. Jac could smell the scent of dirty sewer water wafting off her. Her stomach bucked as nausea crept up her throat.

The bricks parted under the Keeper's touch, unfolding as if mechanical and allowing a small passageway through.

"Hazel, come on," Jac said, grabbing his hand

and pulling them both through the break at the same second the Mourner landed on the ground with a screech. She still stood on all fours, her elbows jutting upward as she scrambled toward them. It was a vision that Jac knew she would never forget, the scuttling, awkward way she came at them. Jac grabbed Hazel, and the two of them ran toward the opening. Once they were through, the bricks knitted themselves back up, finally cutting off the cries of the Mourner.

The silence felt like a gift.

14

THEY FOUND THEMSELVES IN ANOTHER LONG HALLWAY, PANTING AS they caught their breath. Behind them the bricks remained closed up neatly, the Oubliette and the Keeper and hopefully the Mourner all locked on the other side. But Jac knew now, more than before, that the House could not be trusted. Doors would open and close on their own. Walls could be sealed; ladders would vanish. She started to think of herself and Hazel as two tiny mice caught in an impossible maze.

A maze built from her nightmares.

"You okay?" Hazel asked, interrupting her thoughts.

"Yeah," she said softly, nodding. "I just don't trust this place."

"That is the understatement of the century," Hazel said. "Now what?"

Yes, now what? the House whispered in her head.

Was it mocking her?

"Now we keep going," Jac said as she pressed forward, reminding herself the only way out was through. Jac pushed the House out of her head. It was trying to trick her, and she knew that. It had brought the Mourner and the ghosts and all these terrible nightmares that she'd already forgotten about.

Did you forget? the House asked, pushing its way back in. *Did you?*

Jac squeezed her eyes shut and pinched the bridge of her nose, as if that could push the voice away. Now was not the time for this. Now was the time to focus. She needed to find her cabinet, and then they could get out of here. That was the only thing that mattered.

Surviving.

Isn't that all you ever do? the House asked. *What if you just let go?*

Jac kept her eyes shut. "No," she said, louder than she meant. Letting go meant giving up. Letting go meant not fighting. And what was Jac if she wasn't always fighting? If she didn't always have to be better, healthier, stronger, faster.

The Monster from her childhood, the one with the eyes like lamps, flashed before her eyes.

"No," she whispered.

Hazel heard her and gave her a look as they headed down the hall. "Okay, right. We're going to find this cabinet. We're going to get out," he said. He sounded so sure that Jac whispered a thank-you, low enough that he couldn't hear but loud enough that she knew she'd said it.

The hall stretched before them, seeming to go on forever, the light never reaching far enough to show an ending, just a long pinpoint of darkness in the distance and, when they looked back, the same behind them, the Oubliette long gone. The darkness was punctuated by the candle sconces that burned on the wall, showing the light wood paneling and painted portraits.

"Is this the same hallway as before?" Hazel asked as they walked.

"I don't think so. I don't remember those portraits."

"Well, we were busy running for our lives, so." Hazel let out a half-hearted little chuckle.

Jac glanced up at the portraits as they passed. Stoic men. Stern women. Faces that never smiled but instead only stared down at Jac. For a split second one of them looked like her old doctor. She held their eyes, and with a shudder, she noticed that the paintings held hers back. They followed her, eyes shifting as she passed them. When she glanced back, she swore in the sliver of light that was left the faces had changed. No longer stoic and stern but instead snarling. Jagged teeth jutting out of mouths. Vampiric and hostile and watching her.

It's just your imagination, Jac told herself. *It doesn't mean anything.* She wondered how many times she would have to say this before she believed it.

"No hallway can last this long," Hazel said as they walked slowly, the darkness ahead of them stretching. The only light was the twitchy flick of the candles on the walls. Jac felt her fear jumping around inside her, hopping from limb to limb, and for the first time she appreciated it. Being afraid kept her sharp.

And maybe being sharp was the only way to survive the House.

"If we're still underground, which I feel we must be, then this tunnel must go straight back into the woods."

"Wait, what?" Jac said, squinting into the dimness ahead.

"From the Oubliette. We climbed down that ladder. We never went back up. So, we have to still be underground."

"I don't know if the House works that way."

"Well, physics does. What do you mean the house doesn't?"

"I just think it . . . does its own thing."

"It's a house," Hazel said. "I mean, a huge confusing one, but it doesn't have a mind. It isn't in control."

Jac glanced sideways at Hazel and could tell from the sound of his voice that he didn't necessarily believe this either, but she let it go. Something glinted gold at the end of the hall, flickering in the candlelight, catching Jac's eye.

"Something is down there," Hazel said.

They approached with caution, nervous about what the House was offering up next. There was a great gold gate, stretched across the end of the hall like an accordion, and behind it, an elevator.

"Yes!" Hazel said. "This is how we'll get out." He pulled the gate back, and it relented with a weary, metallic groan.

Jac wanted to remind Hazel that in the House doors don't always lead out, but she didn't see the point. He thought he understood how it worked. But Hazel wasn't the one the ghosts were grabbing at. He wasn't the one with the key and the cabinet. It wasn't his story that seemed to be built right into the foundation of this place.

The only thing the House cared about, it seemed, was Jac. And she knew this fundamentally, down to her bones. It was why the House was here, why it had appeared in her dreams, why it had called to her.

And why it had trapped her.

No, the House countered, *you called me.*

"Okay," Hazel said as they got inside the elevator. There were hundreds of knobs. Did each one take them to a different floor? A different room? "We're still underground, right?"

"What about the hallway? Could that have been going up?"

"I don't think so. I think I would have noticed. I think we both would have. Considering how far down we had to go, I would guess we would feel ourselves going up a very steep hill. So, if everything else has been on this level we have to be underground. Now." He studied the panel before him. "I feel like it would make sense if these knobs were laid out like the house. So, the bottom ones would be our level, and the top would be the highest point in the house. If we can get up there, maybe we can signal for help." Hazel reached up for the top knob but hesitated. "But the middle would be ground floors. Even if the doors don't work, if we can find a window low enough to the ground. Something we could break and then get out."

"Haze, I don't think any of this works the way you think it does."

"Well, we have to try something, right? We can't just keep wandering around this place. Not with the

148

Mourner here. Look what happened to Sam and John. We have to try to find a way out. Before we wind up like them."

As if his words were a command, the golden accordion door screeched shut, snapping like a ferocious jaw. The sound scared them, and they leaped out of the way.

"Haze," Jac whispered. There was a brief second when nothing happened. The gate closed, but the elevator didn't lurch into movement. It lasted a beat. And then another. Jac reached out to pull the gate back open, to get out of there before they were stuck. But she was too late. The elevator rocketed upward, accelerating at such a speed that Jac and Hazel were thrown backward.

"This is bad. This is very bad," Hazel said as he gripped the wall, trying to find something to hang on to. There was nothing but smooth walls as the elevator kept accelerating, metal screaming toward the ceiling until Jac was sure they were going to pop right out of the House just like *Charlie and the Great Glass Elevator*. But that was a magical story full of candy and hope and family. This story, the one they were trapped in, was anything but hopeful. It was terrible and too real. It felt like it was going to end only one very specific unpleasant way: with death.

Death is the end of all stories, the House whispered to her.

"Get on the floor," Jac yelled as the elevator continued to scream to the surface. *Just in case we hit the ceiling* was the rest of that sentence, but Jac didn't have enough air in her lungs to get it out. She squeezed her eyes shut and prayed that it would be quick and painless.

The rush of air as the elevator sped up and the metal screaming filled their ears as floor after floor flickered past the golden gate. There had to be a hundred floors so far. None of this made any sense. The House was huge but it wasn't a skyscraper. Where were they going?

When the elevator finally stopped, Hazel and Jac were thrown into the air from sheer inertia and landed with a hard, painful thud back on the floor.

"That was . . . a lot . . . ," Hazel said, before trailing off. The two of them got up, dusted themselves off, and turned toward the elevator door. It was dim and hard to see what lay beyond the golden gate of the elevator. Jac reached out a tentative hand and pulled the gate back. It groaned in opposition. After that there was no other sound but the huff of their breath as they stepped into the next terrible room.

15

THEY STEPPED OUT OF THE ELEVATOR AND FOUND THEMSELVES IN a kitchen. There was a butcher-block table and five chairs. The table was set as if dinner were about to be served. But upon a closer look, the plates were coated in a fine layer of dust. In fact, everything seemed to be coated in dust, including the old woman at the sink with her back to Hazel and Jac. She was petite, and if it weren't for her thin hair barely covering her scalp, she could have been mistaken for a child. Jac and Hazel exchanged a cautious look before Jac motioned that they should retreat. Get back in the elevator. Find another way. Hazel shook his head.

"Come on," Jac mouthed, stepping back toward the elevator.

"No," Hazel whispered. "Maybe she can help."

Frustration grew in Jac, as she realized that no matter how many times the House showed its true colors, Hazel refused to see it. He still thought help was an option. He didn't understand being the only one you can count on. He didn't understand what it was like to lift a burden and carry it on your own.

He doesn't understand survival, the House whispered.

"It's worth a try," Hazel whispered.

Even that faint hush of words was enough to make the old woman stop. She stood very still, and then slowly, almost painfully slowly, as if her neck were not a neck but some kind of rusted screw, she turned her head toward Jac and Hazel.

Jac's stomach went ice cold. Her legs were tingling, as if they wanted her to run. Now. Quickly.

"Well, there you are," the old woman said, offering a toothless smile at them. Her face was a field of wrinkles, as were her thin, long hands. "I thought you'd never get here." Scurrying faster than Jac had expected for her age, she pulled two of the chairs out. "Come, come, have a seat."

She got behind them and started to push both Jac and Hazel toward the chairs at the table.

"We really must be going," Jac said as the old

woman shoved her, rather hard, toward the table. She was surprisingly strong. "Thank you though."

"Nonsense. I have been waiting this whole time for you. Hours and hours. Days and days. Years and years. Millennia after millennia. Eternity after eternity. Come, come, sit. You must eat."

Hazel and Jac exchanged a nervous glance, and Jac mouthed the words "DON'T EAT." They sat down nervously in the chairs, and the old woman started to pull dishes out of the oven.

"Now then, you survived the Oubliette. And the ghosts in the library. You must be hungry. Please eat."

She started to pile their plates with food, hunks of chicken legs and sloppy mashed potatoes, followed by corn and peas. Everything was piled on top of each other in a mess of dripping food, and the sight of it made Jac queasy.

"We're actually fine, ma'am," Jac said softly. "We're just looking to find . . . "

"Ahhhhh." The old lady smiled that eerie grin again and stared at them. She held Jac's gaze for so long that Jac started to worry she'd had some kind of fit. A stroke perhaps. She just stared at them, her head tilted to the side, that strange haunted smile pulling at her face, her eyes unblinking, the pocked empty sockets of her gums, some of which held the deep purple of infection. It seemed to last forever. The only sound was Hazel breathing nervously next to her. Then, as if nothing had happened, the old woman snapped back to life and said, "Yes, your cabinet."

"Yes, ma'am. We're looking for my cabinet."

"The House is a tricksy kind of place, child. Very tricksy indeed. It doesn't come for anyone though. It came for you. Why for you?"

"I . . . I don't know."

"Oh, I think you might. I think you may very well have figured out how this whole thing works. The way it seems to see right inside you. The way it feeds off your feelings. The way it tells you it called you. Like a ghost in the night."

"You wouldn't know where it is? This cabinet?" Hazel asked. But the old woman didn't look at him. Didn't even seem to acknowledge that he spoke. She just continued to stare at Jac. Jac glanced at her friend, fork in hand, who was shoveling a heap of mashed potatoes in his mouth. Jac slapped at the fork, and Hazel mouthed, "What?"

She shook her head and whispered, "Stop."

How could he be so foolish? How could he be so trusting?

"Very tricksy," the old woman said with a wheezy

laugh. "A puzzle House. A Haunted House. A House for you. A House built by you," she said, reaching out and poking Jac right in the chest. She started to laugh, her mouth wide open so that Jac could once again see all the pocked and dark red holes in her gums where her teeth used to be. "Yes, one might say this is the House that Jac built, yes?"

A cold shudder passed through Jac.

"We really must be going," she said, trying to stop her voice from shaking. This woman was unnerving. The way she talked. The way she laughed. The way she stared so hard at Jac. Like she could see inside her.

"Ah, I see it now! I see you as you see you. A ghost," the old woman said with a smile. "That is what you believe you are, no?"

Jac swallowed hard, brushing away the memory of the ghosts, grabbing at her, begging her. The ones that had told her she belonged there with them. The ones that wanted her to stay.

You know the truth, the House echoed in her head. *Admit it. You'll feel better.*

No, Jac thought. She needed to get them both out of here. She was suddenly aware of how unsafe she felt. They shouldn't have come in here. They shouldn't have spoken to this strange old woman. She pushed her chair out and stood. "We're going now."

"NO!" the old woman yelled, and the seat of Jac's chair rammed into the back of her knees, causing her to fall back into it. "You can go soon. Back to your tricksy House, but not without eating."

Suddenly Hazel yelped, put his hand up to his mouth, reached in, and pulled a long, thin canine tooth out, the end of which was still bloody.

"Jac?" he asked, his hand shaking holding the tooth. He checked his teeth, and Jac realized with horror that the tooth he had spit out was not his own.

Hazel spit the food out. Three more teeth flew out of his mouth, landing on the table. The old woman laughed.

A wave of nausea passed through Jac, and she stared in horror at the teeth littering the table and the one that Hazel still held, his hand quivering. The old woman laughed again, harder this time.

"Looks like you already ate, boy," she cackled.

A chill passed through Jac. What did that mean? She looked at her friend and was gripped with fear that he was now in danger. That somehow even though the House didn't come for him, it would still claim him, suck him down, like it did John and Sam, and turn him into a ghost too.

"Your turn, girl." The old woman pointed toward the table, and Jac's gaze followed. Something had changed. Instead of plates piled with food, there was nothing but teeth.

Thousands of teeth. Covering the plates and spilling across the table. Nothing but teeth, some yellowed and sharp incisors, some white, some still bloody. A sickness rose in Jac's stomach, threatening to spill out of her.

"Don't you want to eat?" the old woman said, laughing. A memory flared hot and white in her mind. Her mother, urging her to eat, and Jac fighting it. The way treatment made the food go funny. The way the metal of the fork was all she could taste.

The old woman scooped up a handful of teeth and shook it, and the sound of them rattling against each other made Jac's stomach swirl. She tossed the teeth across the table, and they rolled like dice. Her laugh was so loud, her jaw so wide open, so full of those pocked holes, that it seemed to have come completely loose, the way a snake unhinges its jaw in order to swallow a rabbit whole. Jac looked from her toothless mouth to the table full of teeth, and her stomach flipped.

A guttural noise came out of Hazel. He spat out two more teeth, whimpered, and said, "I'm going to be sick." He looked at Jac, the whites of his eyes wide and quivering as he coughed up another tooth.

The pile of teeth lay on the plate before him, like a nightmare come stuttering to life.

"Jac, what if I swallowed one of them?" Hazel whispered into the hand he kept cupped over his mouth as if to stop another tooth from finding its way out. Before Jac could answer, the old woman started to cackle again. It was a hard, cruel laugh that shook her whole body. It lit something inside Jac. Something sharp and bright. How dare she laugh at them? How dare they put Hazel through this? This was her nightmare, not his. He hadn't done anything wrong. He didn't deserve this.

Maybe you don't either, the House whispered.

She pushed the voice away. How dare the House mock her? How dare it conjure up her nightmares and then tell her she didn't deserve it.

Suddenly the kitchen cabinets banged open, and from them tons and tons of small white things clattered onto the counters, spilling onto the floor. The old woman squealed in delight, clapping her hands together as Jac realized with horror that they were more teeth. Then the refrigerator door was pushed open from the waterfall of yellowing incisors that poured forth.

Jac looked around the room, realizing with horror that this was the kitchen they had been in before, when John had first seen the Mourner. It was no longer dilapidated and dead seeming. Instead, it felt far too alive as the wallpaper started to peel back, revealing the scrawled writing, the message that had been left for her.

For you and you alone, Jac, the House whispered inside her.

She couldn't look away from the letters as the wallpaper rolled down the wall, revealing the message she hated so much: *The House You've Been Entering Always. Welcome Home, Jac.* The lights in the room started to flicker and dim. Jac looked down at the table, and the teeth were covered in dust. It was as if the room was going back to the way it had been before, rotten and broken.

"Welcome home, Jac," the old woman howled with delight. And then much like the room, she also started to change. Her arms started to grow strangely long. Then her legs. She stretched long, insect-like. *No,* Jac thought. *Not an insect. Like a spider.* Then her whole spine contorted and morphed until it seemed like a whole other person was coming out of her. Her face spouted that gauzy fabric from the dark open hole of her mouth. Laughter now started to change into one long, endless sound, louder and higher, until it was nothing but shrieking.

The old woman had become the Mourner.

"Run!" Jac yelled as the Mourner mounted the table, her arms and legs bent at all the wrong angles. She pushed aside piles of teeth as she skittered forward. Her veil still covered her face, but this close Jac could see her dark blank eyes, her wide, screaming mouth set in a perfect circle. The hand that stretched toward her, the gray skin, the filthy broken fingernails that clawed for her. Dishes crashed to the floor and teeth fell clattering as the Mourner crawled toward them. Jac and Hazel pushed their chairs back so quickly they upended, and for a second Hazel almost lost his balance and went backward with his chair. They turned as quickly as they could, the sound of the Mourner's cries ringing in their ears, burrowing into their heads, and then rattling down into their bones. She could feel it in her teeth.

Jac's sneakers couldn't find purchase against all the teeth, and she went down on her hands and knees quickly, and her palms were stabbed by their sharp edges. One embedded itself into her skin as if it still yearned to bite. She pulled it out, and a small pinprick of blood blossomed. The feel of them, all that bone against her skin, made her stomach roil. She felt Hazel's hands on her, pulling her up and forward and onto her feet as they dashed toward the elevator door.

They got inside, and Hazel pushed every button he could find. But the door wouldn't close. The Mourner was getting closer, darting across the floor like a spider, her arms and legs bent at terrible, impossible angles, her mouth open in a never-ending scream, the sound of which sucked all the air out of the room, making it hard to breathe.

Jac's hands shook as she pulled at the gate on the elevator. "Come on," she yelled in frustration, yanking and yanking at the gate, which stubbornly, almost mockingly, stayed open. Hazel gave up punching every button, and he joined Jac. He gripped the gate and pulled, putting a foot up on the wall for better leverage. The two of them grunted and pulled, but the gate was stubborn.

"Come on!" Jac screamed. The Mourner was right on top of them now, and she felt the gate slip forward as it gave way and screeched closed just as the Mourner reached them.

The Mourner launched herself at the gate, her arms slipping through the metal lattice, those terrible clawed hands grasping for Jac and Hazel. For a brief second the Mourner had a grip on Hazel's shoulder before he screamed and twisted away from her. The scratch of her nails dug into the fabric of his shirt and tore it. She continued to throw her body against the metal, her screams still echoing inside that small space. Both Hazel and Jac pressed against the far wall, just out of reach of her clawing fingers. Hazel kicked his foot up and hit the panel of buttons, and the elevator groaned to life. The Mourner pulled her arms out just in time as the elevator descended. They were left then with nothing but her cries following them down the cold, dark shaft.

16

UNLIKE BEFORE, THE ELEVATOR DESCENDED AT A NORMAL SPEED, floors rolling past, and then stopped with a slight unnerving ding as if nothing had happened. They emerged to find themselves back in the parlor. At least, it looked like the parlor.

"Jac," Hazel said. "Do you think . . . " He hesitated as if saying her name would call her forth. "Do you think *she* knows where we are?"

Jac thought about her theory that the Mourner tracked them through fear. As her heart rammed in her chest, she bit her tongue. "I don't know. I hope not. Let's just say no."

Hazel flopped down onto the couch, exhausted

and shaken. "I'm sorry I ate that food."

"It doesn't matter. It would have happened regardless."

"But all those teeth," Hazel said with a shudder. "All those teeth were in my mouth."

"Let's not talk about that. Let's just try and figure out where we are."

"We're in the parlor. Back at the beginning. There's the door that *doesn't* lead outside," Hazel said, pointing.

"Are we sure this is the same room?" Jac asked, studying the space. She thought of the kitchen and how it had changed. The way the old woman called it a puzzle House. Was this the same space? There were the same large cushioned couches and love seats, the same end tables filmed with dust, and the same hardwood floors. The same giant chandelier hung from the ceiling, the same upright organ in the corner, the same spiderweb design everywhere, the wide staircase. And, of course, all the doors. The doors that only led back to this room. Jac couldn't remember an elevator in the last parlor though. If there had been one, she was sure Hazel would have tried it. He'd tried every other door.

She headed across the room to the large rug in the center. She gripped it and started tugging.

"No way," Hazel said. "I'm not going back down

there. I'm not going back to the Oubliette. We just got out."

"I'm not saying we are." Jac grunted as she pulled the heavy carpet to the side. "I'm just checking something." Once the carpet was cleared, Jac's suspicions were confirmed. There was no trapdoor in the floor. There was no way back to the Oubliette even if they wanted to go.

"Wait," Hazel said, getting off the couch. "So, *is* this the same room?"

"Either it isn't but it looks just like it is, or it is the same room and the House changes it. Regardless, the trapdoor is gone but maybe another door will work."

With that comment Hazel perked up. "You mean?" he said, before bolting toward the front door. Jac watched him, feeling the weight of the key in her pocket and all that it meant. Something was wrong. Jac could feel it in her bones. The House was trying to show her something. Trying to tell her something. Something she wouldn't, or maybe couldn't, listen to. She felt for a moment like she understood what the House meant when it said the Challenge Was Accepted.

"Wait," she said softly. She needed a minute to think. If she could just think, she could figure this whole thing out. She was sure of it. It was right there, like a thing just outside her field of vision. The answer to all of this.

But Hazel was already at the front door, already pulling on the knob, and when it groaned open, he yelled in delight.

Jac's breath caught in her throat. Could it be? Could it be possible? Even as she stared right out the front door, past the porch to the road that stretched ahead, to the discarded bicycles that just hours before Jac and Hazel had left on the side of the road. The distant sound of cars drifted through the open door to her ears. The faint chirp of crickets. The smell of newly cut grass. All of it so amazingly *real*.

Surprisingly, Hazel hadn't moved yet. Hadn't bolted out the door. He stood there, his breath coming hard, a weird hysterical laugh starting low inside him and then growing louder until it morphed into a sob.

"Jac?" he whispered, and something inside her broke. How long had they been inside? How long had they been going from room to room to room, frantically avoiding whatever nightmares the House offered? And here it was now, the freedom they craved. Here was the cool evening air. Here was the evening sky. Here was the whole world.

And most important, just through that door, down

the road, and around the corner was home.

Home.

Go, her brain screamed. Go before it all fades away. Before you lose it to this musty, twisted House. Go before the door slams shut and never reopens. Before the Mourner finds you again. Go before the ghosts come and claim you and your greatest fear comes true. Go before this House takes you. She had to get out of this terrible House, filled with her nightmares, the ones that woke her in a sweat. The ones that stared at her through the mirror, reflected in her tired anxious eyes.

Go, her brain screamed. *Just go!*

Her body finally caught up to the voice in her head, and she ran, met Hazel at the door, grabbed his hand, and raced through the doorway. She didn't even feel her sneakers hit the wood slats of the porch, didn't even feel her legs manage the steps without tripping; she just ran, hard and fast, thinking that somehow by some sheer luck they had made it out of the House. They were free.

When they reached their bikes, she slowed down just enough to swoop up her discarded backpack and slip it over her shoulder before lifting the bike and pedaling as hard and fast as she could. She willed the bike, as if it were a horse, urging it forward, begging it to outrun the House's reach. She didn't look back, only once to the right to see Hazel, pedaling along beside her, his breath ragged, tears still running down his cheeks.

They had made it. One way or another, they got out.

The cabinet, the House echoed inside Jac's head. She shook it away. That didn't matter anymore. *You were supposed to leave something behind in exchange. That was the deal. Your Challenge Was Accepted.*

She pushed harder on her bike pedals. None of that mattered. What mattered, the only thing that mattered, was that they were out. They were free. Whatever nightmare they had stumbled into was finally over, and she didn't care how or why. She cared only that it had happened.

But, the House urged. *What about the cabinet? What about the truth? What about the pact . . .*

No, Jac thought. She didn't care about the key or what was in the cabinet. The House was cruel.

You know that isn't true, the House said. *I simply am, as all things. And what is life if not sometimes cruel.*

She pedaled harder, as if she could outrun that voice in her head, just now noticing her cheeks were also wet with tears. But if it was from the wind or fear she wasn't sure. Jac knew that sometimes in life there was only surviving. There was only getting through it.

Right? she wondered. But still something tugged at her, hitched against her thoughts, pulled them back. Something told her that this was not the way out. This was not the way through.

When they turned the corner and started the climb up the hill to Jac's house, they slowed until finally Jac said, "Wait, Hazel, stop."

His breathing was jagged. "What?"

She felt it then, the fear and panic melting off her as the distance between her and the House increased. Then, all she felt was that nagging, tugging thought.

"I just . . . we got out, right? I mean . . . *how* did we get out?"

"I don't know. And to be honest, I don't care." He pushed the pedal of his bike and coasted a few feet ahead. "It doesn't matter. The only thing that matters is that we're out. It's over. That's all I care about."

Jac stopped and got off her bike. She looked back down the road toward the House. "It doesn't make any sense."

"Who cares?"

"But . . . how?"

"What are you doing?"

"What do you mean?"

"Exactly what I said." There was an unexpected

bite in Hazel's voice. "We got out. It's over. What-ever nightmare we were stuck in is over. That's all that matters."

"But . . . "

"No, there are no buts. Now we're going to tell our parents what happened and then, I don't know, go to the police or something. Find John and Sam. Get that house torn down."

Jac understood where he was coming from. She did. It made sense. But the idea of explaining to her mother what had just happened—about being trapped in a Haunted House. The word *Haunted* tripped in her mind. But that was what it was, wasn't it? A Haunted House. A puzzle House. A House that changed and morphed and tricked her. A House that was so much more than just walls and windows and doors. A House that was trying to show her some-thing. She thought of Mr. Nobody and his pact, of the Mourner and her screaming, of the Keeper in the Oubliette and his riddles, of the ghosts and their stories. It all terrified her. But behind that terror there was something else. An inkling that another story was being told. That another truth was wait-ing to be discovered. Mr. Nobody called the House a trial. A confession. He told her she needed to leave something behind.

A truth.

But what was her truth? What was she not telling?

She looked back down the street, and for a brief moment she thought about going back. As crazy as it sounded, Jac actually could feel the House calling her back. Wanting her to finish what had been started. Reminding her that it was here for her and her alone. Mr. Nobody had told her that she'd called the House, and if she'd called the House, it was because she needed it. But how could she need something as terrible as that?

As if he could read her mind, Hazel started to laugh. It was not a joyous laugh. It was a hysterical, high, keening laugh. A nervous laugh. An angry, fed-up kind of laugh.

"No way," he said.

"What?"

"We could have died. We could have died in there, and now you want to go back."

"No, I don't. I don't want to go back. I just . . ." The words vanished in her throat. Because that was exactly what she wanted to do. The House called to her. She could feel it. It had found her. She had found it. They were connected somehow, the House and Jac. She just wasn't sure what it meant.

I came because you called me.

Jac shivered at the voice that did not sound like her own. The voice that still echoed in her mind. *You know what the truth is. You're just hiding from it. You know why I'm here and what is really happening. You just have to face it.*

Jac squeezed her eyes shut. She felt her hands start to shake. Back when she was younger the doctors had warned her mother that the statistics were not in their favor. And yet, Jac lived. Had this time been a gift? Or just a slow trick? Because if the darkness was back, what did it matter?

She was still going to . . .

No, her brain said. *Don't think about it. Don't. It doesn't have to be like this. It doesn't have to end this way.*

But what if it did? What if the story was finished? It was nothing she would ever have control over anyway. Jac squeezed her hands to stop them from shaking. If only she could stop her brain from thinking.

"This is so messed up," Hazel said with a disgust that Jac was not used to. "You're messed up." She was jarred by his comment. It was enough to shake her out of herself.

"What did you just say?"

"You're messed up."

"No, I'm not, Hazel."

"You want to go back. That is messed up! Maybe

stop thinking about just yourself. Maybe stop pushing things. Just be glad we're still alive. It's like that doesn't even matter to you. You could have died. I could have died. John and Sam *might* be dead. Doesn't that mean anything?" He pushed his bike forward, walking it up the hill.

She almost wanted to laugh. Death? Yes, that meant everything. It meant everything in a way Hazel didn't yet understand. He never stood on the edge of the abyss and stared down into its depth. He never woke in the night covered in sweat from a dream about a monster that found him when he was just seven years old. A monster that wasn't going to go away just because the light was on. One that clung to her back, sank its teeth into her, one that she would have to carry with her every day.

But there was no way to explain this to Hazel. Those weren't even things Jac could say out loud. Most days she couldn't even say them to herself.

"Hazel, wait," she yelled after him. "Of course it does."

"No, it doesn't," he spat, turning to look at her. "I followed you in there. I came to help you."

"I never asked you to," Jac said without thinking.

"Ha!" Hazel said with bitterness. "Man, have you ever had one actual friend? Back in California, did you ever have someone you would do anything for?"

"Yes . . . of course." Was it a lie? Jac wasn't sure anymore. What happened to your heart when you had to wrap it in iron just to keep it safe? What happened when just trying to stay alive was all you did? All you had time for?

Illness, Jac knew, was a conveyor belt. Once you were strapped to it, you were never going to get off. The thing about maybe dying was that it didn't leave a lot of room for anything else. Maybe it didn't even leave room for living.

"Okay, well, that's me, Jac. I followed you into that house. I was there the whole time. I was in just as much danger as you. And now that we're out, you want to go back in? It's like you don't even care what happened. You don't care what we risked. Do I have to say it again? We could have died!"

"I don't want to go back in! I just . . . " Again, the words died in her throat. She swallowed. "I just feel like things aren't finished."

"Because you didn't find your cabinet or whatever? Who cares! We're out. The whole point of finding the cabinet was to get out. But here we are. Now we need to tell our parents and go to the police. They can come and burn that horrible place to the ground."

"No!"

Jac didn't mean to yell. She really didn't. It just burst out of her. She just needed Hazel to stop accusing her of things, even if they were partially true. She needed to think. Because even though what Hazel had said was kind of true and the idea of going back was terrible, the thought of something happening to the House terrified her. His suggestion that they burn it to the ground seemed unthinkable. He might as well have suggested that they burn *her*. And on top of that, the other problem was she couldn't tell her mother about what happened. Not today. Not ever. There was no universe in which her mother would understand.

She could never sit down across the kitchen table and tell her mother about the House and about the offer, about the cabinet and the key, about the ghosts and what was written on that paper, about the screaming Mourner. If she did, her mother would take one look at her and then pack her into the car for a drive to the hospital. She would know what it meant. She would see it as a symptom.

Because that's what it was, right? That's the thing that Jac couldn't admit to herself. She felt suddenly that that was what the House wanted her to see. You can lie for only so long before even you have to admit that it was all a fantasy and what that fantasy means.

The House existed just to let her know she was sick again.

But Hazel saw it all too, her brain argued.

"Your mother isn't going to believe you," Jac said. "No one is."

"That's not true. The house is right there. They can go see for themselves. Find out where it came from."

"You honestly think if you sit your mother down and tell her about doors that open to other rooms one minute and a different one the next that she'll believe you? How about the Oubliette? The Mourner? You saw her, right? Skittering down the walls like gravity wasn't a thing. You honestly think she's going to believe you? Those things we saw were not possible, Hazel. They weren't real."

Hazel held her gaze, his eyes hard but clear, and for a moment he faltered. It flickered briefly over his face—a look of confusion mixed with fear. And then, as quickly as it had come, it was gone. "They were real. She's my mother. She'll . . . believe me . . . she has to, right?"

But when he trailed off, Jac knew she had him. And maybe his mother would believe him. Maybe she would think that there were some neighborhood bullies. It wouldn't be the first time for Hazel. Maybe she would be concerned enough to at least drive down to the cul-de-sac and see what it was that her son was going on about. She might give him the benefit of the doubt. The point was whatever Hazel said to his mother wouldn't be seen as a sign or an indicator that things had changed.

That would never be the case for Jac.

Whatever words Jac used would set things in motion. Things neither she nor her mother were ready for. She needed Hazel to keep this secret. To keep *her* secret. Even if he didn't know that was what he was doing.

"Hazel, what happened back there, whatever that was, there's no way anyone is going to take us seriously. It sounds absurd."

"So, what then? We just act like everything is normal. We just let it sit there, that monster house. What if kids go in there, Jac? What if little kids get stuck inside? What then? What about John? What about Sam?"

"I don't know."

"We have to *do* something."

"Okay, fine," Jac said, relieved that the conversation about telling mothers was over. "But whatever we decide to do has to be between us. Just us. No one else can know. Not right now."

Hazel shook his head, his eyes darting around the street. Jac could tell he didn't like it, but he wasn't going to fight her. Hazel never did. "Fine. But we're doing something."

"Okay," Jac said, exhaling with relief. "I promise."

Jac pushed her bike forward, forcing herself not to look back.

"Good," Hazel said, following her. "Then tomorrow I'll just burn the cursed thing down."

"That's illegal."

"That house should be illegal. Also, just because something is legal doesn't mean it's good."

They walked their bikes the rest of the way in silence. When they reached Jac's house they stopped.

"You promise, right?" Jac said. "You promise you won't tell anyone."

"Yes, I already told you. I promise. But you have to promise something too."

"What?"

"That we'll do something about that house."

"Okay," Jac lied. She just needed a little more time to think. To figure out what exactly all this meant. In her mind the torn-up pages from the typewriter fluttered by.

You know what it means, the House whispered. *You just have to face it.*

Jac put out her fist and Hazel bumped it. When he turned and mounted his bike again, Jac felt a small panic. She didn't want him to leave. Not after everything that happened. Not after everything they had just been through. "Hazel, wait!"

He paused and looked back at her. "Thank you," Jac said. "For everything. For getting us out of there."

"Well, I think it was just luck, but you're welcome." He pedaled the bike forward, and Jac watched till he rounded the corner. She pushed her bike up the driveway, stowing it around the side of the house, and then came back to the front door. She reached out for the doorknob and then yanked her hand back.

It was spiderwebbed.

Jac squeezed her eyes shut, trying to will it to go away, and then opened them again.

The doorknob was normal again. *You're just tired,* she thought. *You've been through a lot.*

She turned the knob, opened the door, and stepped inside the house.

The House you've been entering always, the voice whispered.

Jac ignored it. Instead, she called out, "Mom?"

17

IT STARTED TO ALL FEEL LIKE A BAD DREAM. THE MORE SHE TRIED to keep what happened in the House in her mind, the more it seemed to all slip away, sliding right through her fingers, like so much sand. Here in the comforts of her own home, in the warmth of her bed, the familiar sounds and smells all around her, she felt less and less like she had ever stepped foot in that strange world. And Jac wanted to let it go, wanted to let it fade away like a bad dream.

Except, every time she was close, a thought hooked itself in her mind and tugged. A thought that said it had been real. A thought that said she hadn't finished what she was supposed to do. She hadn't found her cabinet. She hadn't left something behind. The House was there because she'd called it. And she had just walked away. She had a strange idea of going back to the House, not now, but when she was an old woman, after her life had been fully lived. Going back then just to prove something. What though? That it was wrong? That she was still there? That she'd lived? Or maybe she would just go back to prove to herself that it had—or maybe, hadn't—happened.

She was in bed, staring up at the ceiling, watching the morning light creep up the walls. It seemed much too bright, much later than it should be, as if she had slept in. Jac pushed the covers back and climbed out of bed. The hardwood floors squeaked under her feet, and for a brief moment she was confused. Didn't she have a carpet? She looked down at her toes and the shiny wood. The image of a blue shag carpet under her bed flared in her mind and then vanished. No, she reasoned. Obviously not. *You're just tired*, she told herself, shaking her head as if that could shake out the sleepiness. She tied her hair back in a long ponytail, threw on her jeans and T-shirt, and padded down the stairs.

Her mother was in the kitchen at the sink, with her back to Jac. She was gazing out the window as she washed the dishes. The running water meant that her mother didn't hear her come in, and for a moment Jac just watched her there, listened to her humming to herself.

It had always been just the two of them. Jac's father had been out of the picture by the time she was two years old. She used to write him letters. She remembered the crayon scrawl, the drawings she did of herself so that he would know what she looked like. The hearts she sketched all over the paper and then, when she learned how, writing her own name. She remembered folding the paper edge over edge and tucking it into the envelope. Her mother would take it then and write down an address that Jac was too little to be able to read. They would walk the letter out to the mailbox, and Jac was always the one who got to raise the little red flag on the side of the mailbox—a sign for the mail carrier to stop and pick up the mail. And then she would wait.

And wait. And wait and wait. And nothing would happen. When she was little, she told herself that her father was a sailor and he was on a great adventure, going around the world. She imagined all her letters piling up at his home, waiting for him to come back. How amazing it would be when he returned to find all Jac's letters. She was sure he would come running to see her with stories of his adventures on the high seas.

He would swoop down and pick her up and swing her around like fathers did on television. They would have so much to share.

But that wasn't what happened. Instead, one day, while she was playing in the living room, she saw her mother sneak outside and retrieve the letter from the box, stuffing it into her jacket pocket. At first, she was angry. She thought her mother didn't want Jac to know her father. She figured her mother was mad at her father for some unknown reason. She even accused her of such. But her mother's face crumpled like a balled-up tissue. And that was when Jac knew.

Her father wasn't out sailing the world. He was probably out there somewhere. But her mother didn't know where. The truth was her father didn't care. He didn't care enough to find her. He didn't want her in his life. Jac always wondered whether it would mess her up if she really thought about what that meant. But she didn't get a chance to think about it before everything else fell apart. That was when the tests and the knocking started. And after that, things like her father not being around didn't seem to matter. The only thing that mattered was surviving. That was the weird thing about having your life split in half like this. Eventually everything siphons down to a pinpoint.

You only have to survive.

Just survive.

"Jac, breakfast is ready," her mother said, suddenly and without turning around. Her voice sounded strange. Deeper. Louder. For a second it sounded as if it was in Jac's head at the same time as when she spoke.

"How . . . " Jac said, wondering how her mother even knew she was there. She hadn't turned around, and Jac hadn't made any noise. It was like all of sudden, her mother just *sensed* her.

"I'm your mother, sweetie," Jac's mom said, turning now with a smile on her face. "I know everything." It was a pulled smile, as if her cheeks weren't naturally lifting but being yanked backward, and it unnerved Jac for a moment. The woman before her looked like a stranger. Or worse, she looked like a stranger wearing her mother's face, using her mother's body. How could everything look so familiar and yet so jarringly strange? She blinked, but when she looked again her mother seemed fine. Normal. Her face relaxed, her smile natural.

"You okay, darling?" she said, crossing the kitchen and tucking a stray hair behind Jac's ear.

"I'm . . . fine," Jac said with a smile that she had to coax into existence. "Why?"

Her mother smiled again, held it for a few extra

beats, and then said, "Well, to be quite frank, darling, you look like you've seen a ghost." She laughed then, a touch louder than normal, before returning to the table. "Come and eat."

A chill passed through Jac. An image of teeth flashed through her mind, and for a second it felt horrifically familiar before fading.

"I'm not hungry," she said softly. She kept telling herself it was just her. She was the one that seemed weird and off. She was the one not processing the world right. But there was still something weird about her mother in that moment that went off like a bell in her mind. Something that told her to pay attention.

The House you've been entering always.

Jac squeezed her eyes to shut out that voice. She held out her hands and watched them quiver slightly. Her mother watched her watching her hands and didn't say anything about it. This was not like her mother, the woman that worried and hovered. Instead, she stood over Jac with that same cold smile and watched her wordlessly.

Something was very wrong.

"Darling, you have to eat breakfast. It's the most important meal of the day."

"I think I'm going to be late for school," Jac said, tucking her hands away.

Her mother gave her a look and then started to laugh. Hard and loud. So loud that it startled her.

"School, darling? There's no school today. It's Saturday."

Jac looked at her. Was that possible? Was yesterday Friday? "What about the scan?"

"What scan, darling? There's nothing wrong with you," her mother said.

The fuzzy memories of being in the House made everything seem unreal, like all her thinking was underwater. She tried to imagine the rooms, but everything was coming up blurry and dim, like trying to focus on something just outside of your view—something you can see only out of the corner of your eye. She remembered a ladder that led to a dark hole. She remembered something terrible grabbing at her, snatching her hair and her clothes and trying to keep her inside. But it felt like a nightmare, and the more she tried the more it faded. It must have all been a dream.

"You are such a silly girl," her mother said, holding a pan and a black plastic spatula. "Eggs?"

Wasn't she just doing the dishes? Jac wondered. She caught a look at what was in the pan, and her stomach turned. It wasn't eggs. Or anything edible. Whatever was in that pan was moving, writhing like a muscle. It looked like a tongue, cut from someone's mouth, squirming in the pan. Jac recoiled in horror. "No!"

"Darling, you love eggs. Scrambled are your favorite," she said, spooning them down onto her plate. Jac looked again, and it was just the yellow fluffiness of scrambled eggs. No writhing tongues. Nothing but regular food. "You feeling okay, sweetie?"

"Yeah . . . I'm . . . " Jac trailed off, feeling the pressure around her temples. It felt like her skull was stuck in a vise, one that kept tightening and tightening. She checked her hands again, and still they quivered. Headaches. Hallucinations. Shaking hands. Just like when she was little. But back then she didn't know what to expect. When she was seven, everything was a mystery.

But now, Jac knew how it went. She knew the storm, and she didn't want to do it again. To be honest, she didn't think she *could* do it again. When the doorbell rang, she nearly jumped out of her skin.

Her mother gave her a sideways look. "It's just the doorbell, Jac. Not going to lie, you're starting to make me nervous." Her mother put down the pan, washed her hands off, and retreated down the hall to the front door. Jac looked at the eggs on the plate. They were completely normal. She picked up her fork and gently poked them. When nothing weird happened, she put her fork back down.

It's me, she thought. Maybe it'd been her the whole time. She could hear her mother talking to whoever was at the door. She should tell her that she was seeing things. Hearing things. She should tell her that there were hallucinations. They would have to go back to the hospital. There would be more tests. They would find out if . . .

And that was as far as Jac could go with thinking about this.

Because truthfully, she didn't want to know. Sometimes it was better to not know. Besides, she told herself, Hazel had seen everything too. It couldn't have been a hallucination if other people saw it. It had to have been real, then.

He didn't see the ghosts, that voice said again. *He doesn't hear me.*

Jac put her hands over her ears as if she could block out the House's voice in her head. She hated the way it thrummed, low and deep. And then, like a movie rolling in reverse, she saw everything. The Oubliette and the Mourner. The ghosts in the library. The doors that led to the same room.

The teeth.

She took a deep breath and whispered the only truth she could cling to at this point. Hazel had been there. He saw the Oubliette and the Mourner. He saw all of it. Picturing the way the Mourner had skittered, spiderlike, down the walls of the Oubliette and then her clawing at them through the elevator door sent her stomach end over end. For a brief moment she thought she was going to be sick.

"He saw all of that." She said it out loud to make it true. *Better haunted than sick*, she thought. Better that.

Better cursed than dead.

"Jac, darling," her mother called from the door. "Hazel is here."

She jumped up from her chair and raced to the door. "Hazel!" she yelled breathlessly. "What are you doing here?" She pulled him into the house, and he looked at her like she had suddenly grown six heads.

"I . . . just thought you might want to go for a bike ride. Or down to the lake." He looked from her mother back to Jac.

"Mom," Jac said, looking at her mother. "Hazel and I are going upstairs. We need to talk."

Her mother looked at her with eyes that held a strange, vapid emptiness. "Of course, dear. But not before you've eaten. Hazel, would you like breakfast?"

"I already ate, Mrs. Price-Dupree."

Jac waited for her mother to remind Hazel to call her by her first name, but instead she turned that blank gaze back to Jac. For some reason it sent a shiver up her spine. It was as if her mother's eyes weren't actually seeing her at all but just knew to look in that general direction. It felt otherworldly. Inhuman, even. There was something about her mother in that moment that made her feel like a puppet. Like someone else was controlling her. After a beat that seemed to last forever, she finally spoke again. This time slower, more precise. Almost, Jac realized, calculated. "Well then, Jac, darling, did you finish eating?"

"Yes. All done. Thank you." The lies came easier than she'd hoped. For a second the image of the eggs as writhing tongues flashed through her mind, and she pushed it away.

"Well, okay then," Jac's mother said. Jac grabbed Hazel's hand and practically yanked him up the staircase.

"Ow! You're going to take my arm off. What's wrong with you?" he protested.

Once they were in her room, she shut the door and started to pace the floor. Hazel flopped down onto her bed. "Why are you being so weird?"

"Hazel, what happened last night?"

"What do you mean?"

"What happened last night? What did you do?"

"Um, the usual stuff. I ate dinner and watched television and went to bed."

"That's it."

"Yeah."

"What did you watch?"

"Why the interrogation, Officer?" Hazel joked. "What is this all about?"

"What did you watch? Just tell me!"

Hazel gave her a pointed look as her voice rose.

"I'm sorry," Jac said. "I just need to know."

"I can't remember," Hazel said, staring out the window. Something out there had caught his attention. "It was probably just something stupid. Some sitcom or something."

"What about dinner? What did you have for dinner?"

"Um, chicken, I think." He sounded distracted. His eyes were still glued to the window.

"You think?"

Hazel got up off the bed and started walking toward the window. Jac kept asking him what he ate and watched last night, but each time he gave a different answer, as if he were in some kind of dream state. Whatever was outside had his attention now.

"Hazel, what's going on?"

"Nothing," he said, but it was barely over a whisper. Jac waited a few seconds, and then quietly and carefully she crept up behind him to see what he was looking at. There, just visible over the rise of trees down the hillside, she could see the tall, dark turret. The high windows. The *House* was right there. Could she always see it from her window? Jac wondered. She must have. Houses don't move, after all. Not on their own. The idea that it was watching them as they watched it sank her stomach like a stone.

"Hazel," Jac said softly, touching his arm. When she did, he jumped.

"What?" He looked as if he'd forgotten she was even in the room.

"I don't remember anything about last night."

"What?" He looked at her, confused and a touch scared.

"I don't remember anything. It's like we went from being on the street to waking up this morning."

"That's crazy."

"No. What's crazy is neither do you."

Hazel turned his eyes again toward the window as if some invisible force were calling him. "I do remember. I told you. We had dinner and watched television."

"But you don't remember anything specific. Your brain is just filling that in. Just assuming because the alternative is too much."

"What is the alternative?" Hazel asked, finally pulling his eyes away from the window. In them, Jac saw fear. Pure, raw fear.

There was a sudden demanding rap on the bedroom door. One that made both of them jump.

18

IN THE SILENCE THAT FOLLOWED, JAC COULD HEAR HER HEART thrumming inside her like a creature frantically looking for safety. A lone bead of sweat trailed down her back. She stared at the door, wondering if the knock would come again.

Hazel glanced at her. "Jac, I think . . . "

But he was silenced again by another series of raps, these ones louder, like machine-gun fire. The knocking just kept coming. RAP RAP RAP RAPRAP-RAPRAPRAP.

Jac felt like her feet were stuck to the floor. She couldn't move if she wanted to. Her mouth went dry. Something was wrong. Something was very wrong.

When the knocking finally stopped, she inhaled sharply, just now realizing she had been holding her breath this whole time.

"It must be your mother," Hazel whispered.

Of course. Who else was in the house? And yet, Jac felt a strange urgency to not open that door. To maybe never, ever go near that door. She looked back out the window, at the House.

Yes, it seemed to say. *We see each other.*

"Jac, maybe we should open the door," Hazel said again. His voice was strained as he motioned toward the handle without daring to touch it. "Before she knocks again and thinks we're dead or have escaped out the window. Also, I *really* would prefer it if she didn't knock like that again."

Jac could hear the forced, casual humor that Hazel was so desperately using to cover over his fear, and somehow, she willed herself to walk toward the door. She eyed the doorknob like it was a wild creature. She noticed, as she reached out for the knob, that her hand was quivering. She was about to turn it when the rapping started again, hard and loud. Jac nearly screamed in fright. Instead, she closed her hand over the knob and yanked as hard as possible, no longer caring for the moment who or what was on the other side of the door. As long as the knocking stopped. That was the only thing that mattered.

When she yanked the door open, standing in the doorway was, of course, her mother. In her hand was a breakfast plate. "Darling," she said. "You didn't finish your food."

"Oh . . . " was all Jac could mutter.

"You said you did but you didn't, which is technically a lie, but I'm willing to see past it, I suppose. Rather strange thing to lie about, after all. Are you feeling okay? Is that why you didn't eat?" Her mother cocked her head to the side, but Jac noticed that her mother's eyes weren't focused on her. Instead, they rolled to the side, toward the window.

Toward the House.

"No," Jac said, a shiver going up her arms. "I feel fine. I just . . . forgot."

"Hmmmm. You forgot. I wonder what else you have forgotten?" she said in a voice Jac almost recognized. That deeper voice. "All the same," her mother continued, sounding more like herself again, "please do eat."

She shoved the plate into Jac's hands and offered Jac and Hazel a stiff smile, a quick goodbye, before she turned and pulled the door shut. Jac stood there for a beat, holding the plate, utterly confused.

"What was that . . . ," Hazel started to ask, but

then trailed off when he looked at the plate in her hand. "Gross!" he yelled, and jumped back.

Jac looked down, and the plate was filled with cockroaches, scrambling over each other. They scattered quickly, their shiny brown shells glinting. When one of them started to race up her arm, Jac screamed and dropped the plate on the floor. Hazel frantically tried to stomp on the bugs that fled.

"Wait, wait!" Jac said. "Hazel, stop."

Hazel looked up. Then back down at the plate on the floor. Instead of roach carcasses littered all over the hardwood, there was nothing but squished egg. Hazel picked up his foot to check the bottom of his sneaker, and that too was covered in yellow smears of scrambled eggs.

"What the?"

"They were cockroaches, right?"

"Yes!" Hazel kept looking around the floor like the eggs were going to transform into bugs. And why shouldn't he? For a moment they had.

"You saw that," Jac said, panting a little. "You saw a plate full of bugs."

"Cockroaches," Hazel added. "What is going on?"

"I don't know," Jac said. She was scared but also strangely relieved. Because whenever Hazel saw the same things she did, it proved to her that even as improbable as it was, this was really happening. It proved it wasn't just her broken brain.

"We should clean this up," Hazel said, scooping the smushed eggs into the wastepaper basket near Jac's desk. Jac bent down to help him, and in a few minutes, they had everything cleaned up.

"So, what *is* happening?" Hazel asked, sitting on the edge of her bed.

Jac paced the floor. "I don't know."

"We can't both be hallucinating," Hazel said, and then, perking up, added, "Wait, do you think there's some kind of gas leak? Something that we can't smell that is causing this. I think I saw a thing about it on television. Carbon monoxide poisoning or something."

Jac looked down at the pile of ruined eggs she had tipped into the basket. "I think something is happening, but I don't think it has anything to do with a gas leak."

"What, then?" Hazel said.

But Jac didn't answer, because she didn't want to think that the nagging, clanking feeling inside her was true. Besides, she knew if she said it out loud it would make even less sense than Hazel's theory about a gas leak. At least gas leaks actually happen.

"Maybe we should go for a walk," Jac offered,

trying to desperately will her eyes to not look out the window. She didn't want to know if she could still see the House.

"I'm not going back there," Hazel said softly.

Jac stopped, set the plate on her desk, and sat down next to Hazel on the bed. "Back where?"

But he just looked at her, a hard look. A you-know-what-I-mean look.

"Where, Hazel?"

"The House."

"So you remember?"

"Sort of? I remember John and Sam teasing us. I remember a ladder and a dark hole. I remember feeling lost and . . . cold. I remember screaming. I remember . . . " He swallowed hard and said, "Teeth."

Jac watched him closely, watched his brain and his heart wrestle the truth to the ground and then watched him try to turn that truth into words.

"I think I'm onto something with that gas leak," Hazel said, letting out a loose chuckle.

"No," Jac whispered. "It happened. It all happened. The House and the cabinet and the key." Jac stopped and touched her pocket, but it was empty. Where was the key? No time to worry about that now. "The Oubliette and the Keeper. The library full of ghosts. The platters full of teeth."

"Stop." Hazel squeezed his eyes shut as if Jac's words had opened a window to a world he did not want to see. A world he couldn't bear to see.

But he had to. She couldn't figure this out on her own, and she knew it. "Hazel, it's all real. We did it. And . . . " Jac paused, considered what she was going to say, and then scrapped it and instead said, "We got out."

"We got out," Hazel whispered. Jac noticed for the first time that his hands were shaking too. "We got out."

"Yes, we did."

"We're not going back," Hazel added. His voice was tight, and suddenly he started to cry. She wrapped an arm around his shoulder, as the weight of everything they had experienced crashed up against him. She understood. More than anyone, Jac knew what trauma could do to you. How you could feel fine one second and then, like your whole world is elastic, something snaps you right back into a nightmare and you fall apart. She knew that was what Hazel was doing and that it wasn't going to be a one-time thing. Jac knew that over time he would sort this out again and again. Just like her mother did. Just like Jac did. Trauma takes so much time to sort out.

When he stopped, after a brief bout of nervous

laughter, Jac said, "Want to go for a bike ride?"

Hazel looked at her with wide eyes.

"To the lake. Not . . . anywhere else. Just down to the lake. We could fish."

"There's no fish left in that lake," Hazel said, wiping at his runny nose.

Jac shrugged. "We could still go."

Hazel smiled. It was genuine smile, and something about it filled Jac with hope. She wasn't sure what had happened at the House. Or what any of it meant. But Hazel was her friend, and he was there through all of it. He deserved a little peace of mind. Something stirred inside her, and Jac knew then she had made a decision without really consciously making a decision. She would return to the House. She had no choice. She could feel it in her bones, a thrumming like it was calling her. She needed to finish whatever she had started. But she would do it alone. Hazel would never even need to know.

Yes, the House sighed in satisfaction.

Jac bumped his shoulder with her own. "Come on, let's go."

She got up, stuffed her feet into her sneakers, and slipped into her hoodie. Hazel made a joke about all the fish they couldn't catch, and Jac laughed at him, reaching for the door. She felt light and balanced. She couldn't remember the last time she'd felt this way. As if she knew there was still a task out there to do, a beast to conquer, but she didn't need to do it now. Instead, she would hang out with her friend. Her very good friend. He deserved this.

Jac yanked open her door, and all the breath left her lungs.

Red bricks filled the entire doorway, knitted together and impenetrable.

They were trapped.

19

SHE DIDN'T KNOW HOW LONG SHE SCREAMED FOR. SHE DIDN'T remember beating her hands against the hard red bricks, but she must have because they burned like she had touched a hot stove. She vaguely remembered Hazel kicking at the bricks, but he now stood beside her, asking her something. What was he asking?

"Jac, are you all right? Your hands . . . " He trailed off. "They're shaking."

She squeezed them, and it felt like every bone inside them popped at once. What was happening?

Hazel shut the bedroom door, and Jac was grateful. To even have just a moment where she wasn't staring at those bricks, even if they were still there, was worth it. It was suddenly hard to swallow. She had never felt so trapped in all her life. Her mind floated backward to a story she had been told about a bad queen who was punished by being bricked into her bedroom. They would slip her food through a slot in the bricks, but she would never see the sky again. Never leave the room. The story had burrowed into her brain like a terrible clawed creature. She had never felt claustrophobic before that story. But ever since she'd heard it, every time she saw bricked-up windows or doorways, she always wondered and worried about who could be trapped behind them.

And now it's me, she thought as the panic scratched its way up her throat.

"I'm going to count to ten," Hazel said. "And then I'm going to open this door, and we are going to go have that bike ride, because whatever we saw before isn't going to be there. Just like the bugs."

He sounded so sure that Jac almost started to laugh. But she stopped herself because she knew if she started to laugh now, she wouldn't stop. She knew that the laughter would just keep coming, harder and harder, until it turned into a scream that never stopped. Until she, herself, became the Mourner.

"Hazel . . ." Her voice sounded like it was coming from someone else.

"It's okay." She could hear him muttering something under his breath, some little prayer or wish, but she couldn't make out all the words. Jac had only one word: *please*.

When Hazel reached out for the knob, she was sure her heart had stopped. As the door creaked open, she knew she wasn't breathing. *Please*, she thought. *Please just let it be.*

And for once the universe heard her and the hall was there, carpeted, with pictures hanging on the walls. She squeezed her eyes shut and then opened them again, afraid when she did the bricks would be back. But they weren't.

"I don't understand," she said.

"Me neither. But I do think we should definitely get someone over here to check for a gas leak," Hazel said. Jac squeezed her hands together, felt the sting from slapping the bricks, and knew that there was no way a gas leak could have caused that pain. The bricks maybe had been impossible, but that didn't stop them from being real.

Sometimes impossible things were very, very real.

They stepped through the doorway together, unsure, like astronauts emerging from the space shuttle for the first time. But it was fine. Everything was normal. They headed down the stairs toward the front door, when something stopped her.

Jac turned, and sitting on the living room couch was her mother. She wasn't reading or watching television or anything like that. She was just sitting there. Smiling at them. Her eyes, still vacant, fixed somewhere just past them. There was a strange fleeting whiff of something in the air. Something that smelled antiseptic. Like a hospital. And behind that, something that smelled like decay. As if something had died, rotted, and then been cleaned up. It was a familiar smell, and Jac's stomach dropped as she remembered that was the smell from the House.

"Mom?" Jac asked hesitantly. "Are you okay?"

Her mother didn't respond. She just kept staring into the distance, that smile starting to look more and more fake. Her skin had an unsettling plastic sheen to it.

"Is she okay?" Hazel whispered behind her.

"I don't know," Jac said softly, not daring to take her eyes off her mother. She reached out nervously, as if her mother were a dog that might bite her, and shook her gently by the shoulder.

Jac's mother snapped her head to the side, looked at Jac's hand and then up at her face. Jac recoiled. There was something about that look. Something terribly familiar. A voice inside Jac reminded her to pay attention.

Another voice, a louder voice, a voice that sounded

like her own, told her to run.

She pulled her hand away. "Mom, are you feeling okay?"

"Mom," her mother repeated in Jac's voice. "Are you feeling okay?"

The plastic smile was still there, and Jac's insides went cold. She took a step backward. And then two more.

"Mom," her mother said again. "Are. You. Feeling. Okay."

"What is happening?" Hazel whispered from behind, the fear flickering in his voice.

"I don't know."

"Mom?" her mother asked again. "You. Feeling. Okay."

It's like Hazel's phone, Jac thought. The way the House mimicked things back to you. Except this was her mother. And they weren't in the House.

They weren't in the House.

They couldn't still be in the House.

Jac's blood went cold.

"Hazel . . . "

"Yeah," he whispered, not taking his eyes off Jac's mom. She continued to stare at them. That plastic smile plastered on her face. That vacant, empty look in her eyes. A face that had always brought comfort now brought confusion and fear.

"You. Feeling. Okay."

"What if . . . " Jac started, and then stopped. *It can't be true. It just can't be true.* She couldn't form the words, couldn't make her lips and tongue go there even while her brain screamed, *You know it's true.*

Suddenly her mother stood up. She leaned forward, her arms reaching out toward Jac as if she wanted a hug. Jac and Hazel both stepped backward.

"Okay?" Jac's mom repeated. "Okay. Okay. Okay." Her voice was getting louder and louder, more and more shrill.

"What is happening?" Hazel whispered, his voice high and light. Panic. That was what Jac heard in his voice. The same panic that now made her heart stutter inside her chest. The same panic that drained everything out of her, sank her stomach, and told her that even though it seemed impossible, there was only one truth here.

"Get behind me, Hazel," Jac said. For a second, she thought he was going to challenge her, but he didn't. He just moved. She could hear a ragged breath coming from him, and she wondered if he knew too. If he knew what was about to happen and didn't want to believe it.

"Mom? Is that you?"

"Okay, okay, okay," her mother said. Then her arms started to grow, right in front of them. They stretched and lengthened. Her legs followed. "Okay. Okay. Okay."

If Jac could have, she would have screamed. Instead she just stared in absolute horror, her blood running cold, ice sloshing in her belly. Her brain both told her this couldn't possibly be happening and that of course, yes, this was happening. Because the truth was obvious.

"Okay. Ohhhhh. Kay. Ohhhhhh. Kay. Ohhhhh-hhhhhh."

Hazel whimpered behind her and Jac turned to him. She studied his face for just a beat, the panic that lay in his eyes, the terror that was creeping up his throat. For a second, she was thankful, yet again, that he was here. Thankful she wasn't alone as she said the one thing she knew he didn't want to hear.

"Hazel," she said, surprised by how calm her own voice sounded. "I don't think we got out of the House."

He looked at her briefly before his eyes were pulled back toward Jac's mother, who was now lumbering over the coffee table, skittering like a spider toward them. The low howl of the Mourner oozed from her mouth as she morphed into that creature in that dress and veil. Jac pushed Hazel toward the front door, yanking it open and shoving him outside.

Only there was no outside. There was just the long dark hallway, the flicker of sconces, the portraits that snarled and morphed.

There was only the House.

20

HAZEL WAS GONE.

She ran like she always did.

Except this time, Hazel was *gone*.

Like she had been running in one way or another since she was seven years old. She ran—alone now, so terribly alone—from the nightmare that chased her. From the dank breath and the hands that wanted to catch her and hold her and keep her.

She glanced back still, yelling Hazel's name, but the hallway behind her stretched into emptiness, diminishing to a pinpoint. Her home was gone. Her mother was gone. The Mourner was gone. And now, even Hazel was gone.

She was alone in the House.

She thought back to just moments ago, in her living room, about how she and Hazel had turned, together, to watch everything normal and welcoming transform into something terrible. About how the front door had been open and she had pushed him out and how she'd wound up in this hall alone. Had she pushed him out of the House? Is that what had happened to Sam and John? Was this place truly and horribly just for her?

Before she even had a chance to catch her breath, to think about what to do next, the room morphed around her. The walls seemed to stretch upward like taffy, the wallpaper warping and bending as it did. The ceiling seemed impossibly high. And the floor twisted, slanting at an angle that made no sense. It was disorienting. Jac tried to run but even that seemed impossible. There was no purchase. Her sneakers wouldn't grab on to anything. It felt like the whole House was tipping backward, like an open mouth, and she was going to fall back into the depths of it. She was going to get swallowed up by the House and never return.

Then the perspective changed yet again. This time the floor angled down instead of up, so instead of her sneakers slipping backward she started to stumble forward, moved by her own inertia, tumbling toward an inevitable end. If she could have screamed, she would have. But there was no time for that. Because even though the Mourner was not there, her shrieks followed Jac. It was just her voice, the essence of the Mourner; that was all that was left. Without a body, she was everywhere and nowhere. For a brief horrible moment, Jac was sure that she had become the Mourner, doomed to roam the halls of the House. Jac squeezed her eyes shut and then opened them, half convinced that she would be looking through the gauzy veil of a shroud, that her arms and legs would be bent at impossible angles, contorted and wrong, her hands curved like claws. That she would skitter like a spider across the floor and up the walls.

She would become the very thing that haunted her.

Yes, now you know, the House whispered.

But that didn't happen. Instead, she saw only her hands, her arms, her body, her black T-shirt and jeans, her sneakers trying to find their way down this impossible hall. But the screaming hadn't stopped, and it filled Jac's ears, thumping into her brain, down her nose and throat like so much water she couldn't swallow. The sound filled her completely until she thought she might explode. There was another sound, louder than the scream, a voice yelling no. A voice saying stop. A voice that refused to be silenced.

"STOP!"

And then everything did. The sound vanished, the cry of the Mourner stopped like someone had ripped out headphones, and Jac froze. Her breath panted, ragged and wheezy. Her eyes darted around the hall as she realized with a start that *she* had in fact been the one screaming for it to stop. She had done it. The screaming of the Mourner had been too much, too overbearing, so she'd demanded that it stop. And then it did. She did that. For one brief moment, her anger and fear morphed into something that held power. Something that beat the House.

Are you afraid of me too? she wondered. Because if anger was a weapon, if pain was a sword, Jac had an unlimited supply. That's what happens when your life, your very existence, is held up to the universe for questioning.

You know why you're here, the House said, its voice echoing through her skull. *You have to face it eventually. The only way out is through.*

She took a breath and then another. She held up what was previously fear, looked at it, and watched it morph into anger. It settled over her shoulders like armor. It was both a sword and a shield, something that could both attack and protect. This felt good. Usually, her anger was something that rattled around inside her, sometimes in front of her where it snapped its metal jaws at others, sometimes behind her where its jaws closed down on Jac herself. But right now, it felt like a superpower. Something that cast a bright and shining light against all the darkness of the House.

You called us, the House said. *You keep forgetting that.*

Jac gritted her teeth. Regardless of what other lies that House told, she would never believe this one. She didn't ask for this. She didn't want this. All she wanted was to go back home. Her true home. At the idea of being locked up, her anger started to sing. She let it fill her, let it invade every inch of her, relishing its power. Anger was good. Anger was productive. She felt it lap away at fear and terror, leaving her nothing but the white-hot light of a stripped-down nerve that would get her out of the House. She felt cleaned out. Hard. Tough.

She wondered why people always got upset when kids were angry. Adults were always shutting that down. Always telling kids to be nice, to be friendly, to eat up their anger in so many bites. Telling them to make friends all the time as if they didn't deserve to fight for what they wanted too. As if that kind of passion belonged only to grown-ups. As if anger were something they weren't entitled to, a currency that didn't apply to them.

But Jac was angry. And this anger felt good.

Focus, her newly sharpened brain told her. *Focus on what matters.*

Ahead of her, the seemingly endless hallway revealed an end. Jac stood in front of a black door. She glanced behind her and watched the hallway stretch into darkness.

The only way out is through, she thought as she turned the squeaky knob and let the door swing open. Jac looked around at the room she found herself in. The first thing she noticed was the smell, that dank, watery, mildewy, rotting smell. Like there had once been considerable water damage.

Figure out where you are, her anger said, *and figure out what comes next and face it.*

Yes, the House whispered in her ear. *It is time to face it.*

The only piece of furniture in the room was a small end table upon which sat an old-fashioned red phone. The kind with the big handle and cradle and the buttons that you hooked your finger into and then turned on a spindle. On the opposite side of the room stood another black door.

The walls were strangely spongy and porous. Jac reached a tentative hand out and with her index finger pressed against the wall. It gave way under her touch, pushing inward like a bubble she could pop. When she let it go, it inflated back into place. From the depression her finger made, a small trickle of dank-smelling gray water started to leak. It dribbled in a long, slow crawl down toward the floor. The yellow wallpaper was peeling, warped and wet from all the moisture in the walls. Jac could feel it too, the way the air felt heavy, like it did just before a big summer storm was about to break. The humidity was oppressive, and she began to sweat through her shirt. Her mind went to the ghosts in the library, the way they were all wet, water bubbling out of their mouths and running down their faces. A small bead of sweat cascaded down the side of her face. She wiped at it quickly as if that would erase it. Is this how it started? Sweat that turned to water? Was she turning into a ghost?

Somewhere a bell tolled. She could hear it echoing through the house, the gong ringing through the walls. She thought of the parlor, the library, the Oubliette, the sound of the bell echoing through all those spaces, searching the House until it found her. What would happen if she did not find her cabinet? Would the House turn her into one of those ghosts? Would she be another sad, angry haunt at a typewriter, reliving the worst thing that had ever happened to her? Would she be like the others, desperate to claw her way back into life? Hysterical to be defined by something else?

No, her anger told her. *You will not become that. You will not lose this.*

Yes, you will, the House offered.

No, she thought.

Yessss, the House whispered. The hiss of the *s* rolled around her skull.

"No," she said aloud with conviction. Not yet. She still had time to finish this. The weight of the key was back in her pocket. She had to find the cabinet, face whatever was in there, leave behind her truth, and then get out.

And when she did, just like Hazel had said, she was going to burn it to the ground.

She suddenly and deeply missed him. She felt it all the way down in her bones. Where was he? Was he home, maybe asleep in his own bed, having a fever dream about all this? Was that what had happened to Sam and John? Jac wished it was true. She wanted that for him. She wanted him to be free. The House wasn't here for him. He could still be a kid in the way that Jac couldn't. In the way she hadn't been able to since she was seven.

Since it was taken, the House said.

"Be quiet," Jac said, her voice a hard whisper. She didn't sound like herself. She sounded older. More honest. She sounded like someone who was ready.

Ready to face the truth, the House added.

But hadn't she always? That had been her last five years. While everyone, her mom, her teachers, her new friends, had wanted her to pretend, she knew the truth. A normal life, becoming the Old Jac, that had just been pretend. Jac couldn't go back. Part of dealing with Everything You Went Through, as her mother liked to call it, was accepting that your body didn't work the way it was supposed to. That something had gone off course. That one little cell inside you went rogue and then bubbled up to more and more until your hands didn't work right.

And the real truth? The real truth, the one that Jac thought of every day, was that it could happen again.

But that was something she wouldn't—*couldn't*— talk about. Not to her mom, and not even to Hazel. But sometimes, late at night, the words scurried out of her mind, flitted across her tongue, and dared to come to life.

And sometimes when she was brave, she dared to whisper: *What if?*

You want to confess, the House said.

Jac shook her head to clear it. She wanted that

voice out of her head. She hated the way it heard her thoughts and twisted them. Her anger sang again, hard and real like a weapon that could protect her.

Jac lifted the key out of her pocket and squeezed it tight, thinking about the rules. She had to find her cabinet before the Mourner found her. Leave something behind. She wasn't sure what that meant. She couldn't imagine what the House would want that she could possibly give. She had nothing to leave behind.

Nothing but the truth, the House said. *Nothing but* your *truth.*

But Jac still didn't know what that meant. Or if she did, it was only an inkling, an idea of a thought and not something she could put into words. Not something she could confess.

Jac crossed the room, determined to keep going forward, and reached out a tentative hand, fearful that if she opened the door, she would be washed away in a tidal wave of terrible water. That it would drown her and ghost her and end her. She reached for it, knowing she had to keep moving forward, and just as her fingers touched the glass doorknob, she heard her name.

"Jac," something whispered. "Jac, can you hear me?"

She spun around but there was no one in the room.

The voice didn't sound like the voices in her head, neither the one the House used nor her own. It didn't sound like the scream of the Mourner. For a second, she thought it sounded like the ghosts that haunted the library, but then she realized that wasn't it. It sounded familiar and soft like a friend. With a shock she realized it sounded like Hazel.

"Hazel," she called. "Is that you? Can you hear me?"

"Jacccccc." His voice sounded farther away now, like it was crossing the room. She took a tentative step forward, nervous that the House was trying once again to fool her. But it *was* Hazel. She was sure of it. It was her friend. Her only friend. With each careful step forward, she followed it.

"If that's you, Hazel, keep talking. I'm trying to find you," Jac said. "Please, just keep talking."

"Jacccccc," his voice echoed again, seeming to come right out of the wall itself.

"Hazel? Where are you? Can you hear me? Are you in here? Are you still in the House?"

His voice rose and faded, like a radio coming in and out of range. "Jaccccc."

"Hazel!" She screamed his name this time, panic clawing its way up her throat. "Hazel, where are you?"

She reached a tentative hand up toward the wall,

which was where it sounded like his voice was coming from. Was he on the other side? Trapped in another room? The wall was no longer just water damaged and spongy. It was now running with water. It gushed down the wallpaper and pooled at her feet. "Hazel?" she whispered.

Suddenly a face pushed through the wall. A gauzy face. A veiled face. She could see the impression of the eyes and the long open O of the mouth. The hard angle of the nose. Jac shrieked and fell backward, her arms automatically going up to shield her face. When she looked up, the face was slowly starting to fade back into the wall, and her stomach did somersaults.

Was that Hazel? Was he was somehow trapped *inside* the walls?

"Hazel?" she said softly. "Can you hear me?"

She got up and walked carefully over to the wet, spongy spot in the wall where the face had tried to push its way through. The way the wallpaper had stretched around his features gave Jac a chill. How could he breathe? Was he okay? A cold thought passed over her. Was Hazel getting turned into a ghost?

She pressed her hand against the wall again, and when it yielded under her touch, she snatched it away, fearful. But then she let her anger swell inside her, sharpened it to a blade, and used it like the only weapon she had left. She laid the palm of her hand flat against the wall and pushed. The wall stretched before her, pulling like taffy, enveloping her whole arm. She was terrified, but below that simmered a small flame of hope. Hope that Hazel was on the other side. That he was there and he would take her hand and she would somehow pull him back through to this side. That she could save him.

Save yourself, you mean, the House whispered in her head.

Something cold wrapped itself around her hand, and she gasped. The grip was freezing and firm, and she knew instinctively that it was not Hazel. Whatever had her was strong, and when it pulled her arm sank even farther into the wall.

"No," she whimpered.

She placed her other hand against the wallpaper and tried to find purchase so she could push back, but it wasn't working. She was getting sucked farther and farther into the wall. The stretched wallpaper was now up to her armpit. Her body and her cheek were pressed against the wall, threatening to follow her arm. Inside she could feel the tug of many hands, not just one.

It wasn't Hazel, she realized with horror. *Oh no. What have I done?* She strained and pulled against those hands, her mind going back to the ghosts that caught at her hair and her shirt. Hungry ghosts that wanted to keep her here and eat her up. More faces pressed themselves through the spongy walls. Empty eyes. Wide mouths. Sharp teeth.

"No!" she screamed again, throwing all her weight back until she felt the grip of those fingers relent as she pulled herself free. She landed hard on her back and then quickly scrambled away, pressing her back up to the opposite wall, holding her right arm, the one that now felt so horribly cold, so horribly weak.

So horribly dead.

Jac took a breath and then another one. From behind her, she felt a hand grab her shoulder, and she screamed and scurried away from that wall. She watched another hand try to push its way through, trying to find something to grab on to.

"Jaaaacccccc."

It's not Hazel, she told herself. The House was trying to fool her. The ghosts wanted to pull her into the walls and turn her into one of them. They were using Hazel's voice to trick her.

He never belonged here. He isn't the one who called us.

"Good," Jac said, her voice froggy. "That means he got out. Good for him."

Suddenly the red phone in the corner of the room

rang, a bleating, jarring noise. She eyed the walls, but they had settled down now. No more faces. No more hands trying desperately to pull themselves out of death. She walked over to the phone and then looked up at the door. She should just go. She shouldn't answer it. But it kept ringing, loudly, glaringly. Finally, she couldn't take it anymore, and in a fit she yanked the phone off the cradle and placed it to her ear. She braced herself for the wail of the Mourner or a voice that mimicked her own or Hazel's but instead it was just a steady knocking sound.

Like the Machine. Or a bomb. The knocking stopped, and there was a blast of an air horn so loud that Jac pulled the phone away from her ear. Her heart was thrumming in her chest, beating out a frantic pace, but still she heard it. The knocking had stopped and now there was something else. She opened her eyes slowly and with a shaking hand put the phone back to her ear.

"Hello?" Jac said softly, her voice hoarse with fear.

"Hello, Jac. Are you going to come find me?" the voice asked, followed by a giggle. It was a child's voice. She was sure of it. "Are you coming to save me?"

"Who is this? Where are you?" she asked, but the kid only giggled again before the line clicked and the steady drone of the dial tone returned. Jac placed the receiver back on the phone and took a deep breath.

Find your anger and use it, she told herself. It was a sword and a shield, and it would carry her through this. It would get her to her cabinet, and then it would get her free. A feeling started in her chest, warm and strong, another light against the darkness. It spread to her legs and arms, filling her whole body with a strength that cleared her head and quieted her heart. She realized she could do this. After everything she had been through, she would not let this House beat her. Her body might have been through trauma; it might have survived pain, but it was still here. She had legs that walked firmly without hesitation toward the door. Arms that reached out, grasped the handle, and pulled the door open. She had a solid, beating heart and a quick-thinking mind that told her it was okay to step over the threshold. She was a girl. A girl with power. A girl with fear, yes, but fear that morphed into anger and became a thing she held tight in her fist. Not fear that held her.

A girl that walked, head up, heart beating, right into the darkness.

21

SHE STRAINED HER EYES TO GET A GRASP OF THE SPACE, BUT THE room was so thickly dark it swallowed light, even licking up the small shaft that came from the door she passed through. When it creaked shut behind her, cutting off any light, she froze. All Jac could hear was the steady, accelerating pound of her heart. The silence and the darkness combined to feel like a creature of some sort. Something that had been waiting for her. Something that called her. Was this the dark heart of the House? Was this where she would find her cabinet?

She took a tentative step forward, her arms in front of her, desperate to touch something but also absolutely terrified about what that something could be. She turned around, reaching for the door she came through, hoping to find another way out but, as always, the House had other plans. That door was already locked.

Figure it out, her heart hammered.

In the dark, her fingers butted up against a wall. She followed it to the corner, her hands fluttering up and down the wood, like a lost bird, looking for a latch, an anything, that would help orient her. She'd never known such a deep, intense darkness before. It was thick and warm like soup. There was an odor in this room too. Something earthy, a heavy sort of musk. Almost like a wet dog. She reached the corner and followed the angle of the next wall, groping her hands along, unable to see in all this deep, dark black.

She paused, her ears straining. She held her breath and listened.

She heard it again.

A slight tremble of the air, a static whoosh of sound, and she realized with a cold wash of fear what it was.

Breathing.

Raspy. It sounded like snakes slipping through tall grass, a quick sort of danger.

Not her own breath. No. Someone—some*thing*— was in this room with her. That something was what she could smell.

Jac froze in a panic. Her brain rattling off ideas.

Run, it said.

Freeze, it thought.

Go, it pleaded.

Wait, it finally said. *Wait. Breathe and wait.*

Darkness never stays totally dark. Give it some time and your eyes will always adjust. Eventually you can see what is really happening and who, or what, is really in here. Trust that the dark is your friend. Trust in its cover.

She waited, breathing as quietly as possible. She strained her ears to hear the steady inhale and exhale of whatever lurked in the dark with her. There was no change in the breathing, no reason for her to think she had been discovered, and yet Jac felt exposed.

You know who is here, the House whispered to her. *You knew at one point you would face this.*

The Mourner? Jac wondered. No, the Mourner cries all the time. This is a different creature.

A resting creature, the House said. *Until it is not anymore. And when it is awake, it will give chase.*

Jac's blood went cold. Her limbs started to tingle. She felt all the very small hairs on her skin stand on end at once.

She squeezed her eyes shut as if that could change the darkness. As if that inside darkness was different than this outside darkness. She did it if for nothing else than to try to blot out the terrible voice of the House in her head.

You have to face this. This is why you called me.

I didn't call you, Jac thought. She wanted to say it. She wanted to scream it. She wanted to scream like the Mourner screamed until her throat was raw and rotten. To scream forever the way the universe goes on forever. She wanted to dissolve into that scream, wipe this House away, and free herself. The desire to do this, to make so much noise that the world would have to acknowledge her, thrummed inside her, its beat matching her stuttering heart.

For all the unfamiliar horrors the House had manifested, Jac knew this Monster. Knew where its horns were, what its breath smelled like. The terrible light that burned from its eyes. The way its hooves sounded when it ran, the boom of it rattling her bones. And run it did.

The Monster always chased her. Had since she was seven years old. Its hooves sounded like the knocking of the Machine in the Cold Room. Its breath smelled like a stranger, metallic. Antiseptic. Its eyes shone like two large lamps that she couldn't hide from. It ran all the time. It ran and it chased Jac, and sometimes it morphed into a doglike thing with teeth that would get so close that Jac knew if she slowed down at all, they would close around her leg or her heel and she would never, ever get free. The Monster was always hungry. The Monster never wanted to let her rest, and it would never, ever let her forget.

She had to get out of this room without waking that thing. Jac felt along the wall, moving silently, her hands searching for the door that had brought her in here. There was nothing but smooth wall and the steady breathing of the thing in the room with her.

How could it be here? The Monster was a nightmare from when she was little. It wasn't real. The Monster and the Mourner were just bad dreams, and bad dreams couldn't really hurt you.

But what was this House if not a collection of bad dreams?

Somewhere in the dark she heard the Monster stir. She froze. She would wait it out, wait until its breathing resettled, and then she could continue to search for the door, and she could get out of this room.

And then she had another terrible thought. What if this room held her cabinet? What if it was right behind the Monster and she had no choice but to face it? Isn't that the way it works in stories? The dragon is always guarding the treasure.

Jac shook her head. But this wasn't a story. This was her nightmare come to life, and she didn't know what to do with a nightmare.

You face it, the House said. *That is the whole point of a nightmare. To face the monster.*

Anger flared hot and white inside her. It wasn't fair. She'd already faced a monster. Everything she had been through wasn't fair. The tests and the surgery and the pills. The years they stole.

The Monster in the room stirred.

Jac was angry, and in the dark her anger morphed into a sword. Something she could use to kill the Monster. She thought of the assembly line she was strapped to, full of doctors telling her words she didn't understand, full of her mother's tears, full of sharp needles and IVs and the steady beep of machines. An assembly line she didn't want. When other eight-year-olds had been out playing, she had been inside resting. Always resting. There was always going to be another scan, another test, another chance for six months to go by and a doctor to tell her she was either okay or not okay. Every six months, her life was put on hold, and then if the universe decided she was worthy she would keep on going.

Somewhere in the room, the Monster growled low and long.

Sometimes the anger was so hot, so all consuming, that it stopped feeling familiar. It tipped away from anger and into something more. Something that had once made her break the chair in her bedroom. She didn't even remember doing it. One minute she was sitting there, thinking about things, and then the next she was a crying, panting mess, panicked and scared, standing over the shattered remains of that little wooden chair. She must have smashed it against the wall, because there were pieces on the other side of the room too. She had broken the ceramic box on her dresser. It was a gift from her mother, and when Jac saw it lying there she was overcome with guilt.

When her mother came upstairs, she held Jac. She said things to her, but Jac couldn't remember what they were. She felt only the white, hot pain. It was then that she realized that if she wasn't careful, the anger that filled her, that made her brave enough to swim in the crater lake and to stare down monsters, could also tip and tumble into something uncontrollable. The anger could turn into rage. Rage was more than she could handle. And here, now in this room, she felt the rage tingling through her body, threading around her limbs, threatening to take control.

And the Monster felt it too, felt that rage like sugar on its tongue, and it opened its eyes. They shone white-hot light, like a spotlight that fell upon Jac. It was like staring into a car's headlights, and her eyes burned with it. It was exactly like her nightmare. As if now, after all this time, the universe finally saw her and decided it did not like what it saw.

She squeezed her eyes shut.

No, the House said. *You must not look away.*

The Monster heaved upward, and though she could barely see it she could feel its size. It filled the room. It smelled terrible. It took a shuddering step forward, and Jac heard the hard-echoing stomp of its hoof. The rough snarl of its low growl. It stared at her; the light that came from its eyes blotted out all other things so that Jac could see it only in snippets. A horn here. A hoof there. The long, raggedy fur that hung in clumps from its hide. A long, wet fang jutting from its mouth.

It moved toward her, and she knew that even though it was large and seemed lumbering that once it started to run it would not stop. There was nothing left in her lungs for the scream she felt inside. The anger she'd had before, the one that felt like a weapon, was gone. It seeped out of her once those eyes were on her. It belonged to the Monster now. The creature siphoned everything out of her, leaving only fear. Fear is what the Monster fed on. It wanted to eat her up. It couldn't live without her.

She gave it life.

The Monster looked around the room, the light from its eyes casting across the space, showing Jac chairs and couches and wallpaper. Everything but the one thing she needed. And then just before the Monster settled its light back on her, she saw it. Just behind the Monster was a door. All she needed to do was get there.

The Monster turned its head down, like a bull, and those sharp, thick horns glinted. It opened its jaws and howled a terrible, thunderous cry that Jac felt in her bones. She remembered that sound. She hated the House now more than ever. She hated the way it pulled from her childhood nightmares this terrible hulking beast.

We must not look away, the House said.

In response to the Monster's terrible cry, Jac let out a scream of her own. It felt good, the way the air rushed through her lungs, the way the sound filled the room. She wished it could last forever, but she knew it wouldn't. But it was enough. Enough to get her limbs tingling, enough to fool her heart and her mind into doing this incredibly stupid idea.

She pushed off the wall and she ran right toward the Monster, staring right into the beams of its eyes. She ran hard and fast, and as she got closer, she could see the open maw of its mouth, the way its jagged teeth flashed, yellow and dripping. The way its tongue roiled in its mouth, waiting for her, hoping for her, desperate to swallow her. And just before she landed inside that mouth, at the last possible second, as her feet pounded across that hardwood floor, she ducked to the left.

The Monster's jaw shut with a terrible sound like a steel cage slamming. She dodged past one great hoof that lifted and tried to stomp her out. She faked and weaved past its long, knotted hair, past its rough hide. She kept her eyes trained on what was now just a blot of slightly lighter dark against deeper dark.

The door.

The Monster roared again and turned. It reared up on its hind legs, and Jac wondered how this room could be big enough to fit it. How could the House even be big enough? It was huge, this Monster. Huge and loud and dangerous. If she could just get through the door, she could get away.

She ran, hard and fast, and as she slipped through the door, feeling like she was going to make it, like she was free, she glanced back. The doorway grew and stretched, first tall and then wide. The House opened for the Monster, giving it free range down its dark halls. The horror of it filled her. She hated the way they worked together. With each steady pounding footfall, the Monster chased her. Chased her right out of the room and down the next dark corridor. She ran frantically, arms pumping, chest burning, knowing that the steady thwack of the Monster's hooves behind her were increasing, that it was closing the distance, that if she glanced back, its terrible teeth would be right there. Just inches from her.

And once it got to her, it would eat her up, and then, she realized, this would all finally be over. And she felt something stir, some small kernel of relief. The idea that it would all be over, that she could put down this heavy nightmare, that she could just walk away into the nothingness, felt like a gift.

No, her brain screamed. *You want to live. You want to live.*

And that truth pushed her farther, pushed her tired limbs past the point of exhaustion. Living mattered. She had already worked so very hard to stay alive.

She turned a corner and crashed through another door, the Monster roaring behind her, so loud she wondered how the walls could stay upright.

22

THE WALLS GAVE WAY TO GLASS—FLOOR-TO-CEILING MIRRORS, IN fact. It was so startling that when Jac first saw her reflection she held her arms up to cover her face, sure it was someone else, terrified it was a ghost. She hit the glass hard, having been running so fast, and landed even harder on the floor. She was surprised it didn't shatter and cut her to ribbons. Dazed and panicked but still okay, she managed to pull herself up. She spun around, expecting to see the lamplight eyes, horns as pale as scars, and ragged fur . . . but the Monster was gone.

Jac quieted her breathing as much as she could. When she was younger and the Monster was just a thing of her dreams, the only escape was to wake up. She would do so sweat soaked and shivering, crying for her mother, who would come running to hold her and calm her. Her mother would kiss Jac's head and rock her in her arms, letting her know that she was there and that nothing would ever hurt her. What she wouldn't give right now to be able to open her eyes and find that same comfort. That was the best part of being a little kid. It was strange to think there had been a time when all she'd needed was her mother to make her feel safe. Even when the Monster turned real. When had that changed? Over the years, even with it just being the two of them, things had begun to feel strained. Jac loved her mother, but she also couldn't stand the way she worried. The way everything was a sign of things going bad. The way she panicked if she didn't know where Jac was all the time. The constant texting, the calls. But most of all, it was the way she looked at Jac like she was a doll that was going to break.

Or was already broken. The way she felt less like a daughter and more like a patient.

Yes, the House said. *This is why you're here.*

Its voice was enough to shake Jac out of herself. She looked around the room, if it could even be called a room. It was more of a maze, corridors all made of mirrors like a giant labyrinth. She glanced back at the door she'd come through, peering down the long, dimly lit hallway. She saw no sign of the Monster. Heard nothing. Smelled nothing.

She took a breath and pulled herself to her feet. At the right angle she could see herself replicated over and over again in all the mirrors around her. She lifted her hand, and her reflection did the same.

Sort of.

The reflection right across from her did it at almost the same time, but the one behind that was another second behind, and so on until the farthest image of Jac took some time to lift its hand. She rubbed her eyes and tried again with the other hand. But the same thing happened. There was just a little beat, a hiccup of a pause. It made her feel like she wasn't looking at her reflection but instead she was looking at another version of herself. Hundreds of them.

She shivered though it was not cold. Looking at herself like that, it felt like she was seeing all the different Jacs, from all the different versions of this story. The ones that never got sick. The ones that died. It was hard to tell which Jac was the real Jac and which one was a reflection. For a moment she felt like she was the reflection of the Jac across from her, and when that one smiled at her she had to touch her own face to be sure that she too was smiling.

She heard something then. The steady thwack of hooves. Smelled it too. The wet-dog musk. The low steady growl.

The Monster.

Jac slipped behind the open door, catching her reflection doing the same. She pushed it closed almost all the way, peering not through the opening but through the crack where the door met the bracket. Her breath was warm on her face.

It took a few minutes, but she saw it: the steady, low beam of light as the Monster's eyes searched the hall for her. She tried to push the door the rest of the way closed, knowing that the Monster had only hooves and couldn't open the door.

But it could kick down the door, her brain countered.

Still, she pushed the door closed, and it started to squeal on its hinges. Loudly. So loudly that the light from the Monster's eyes fell upon Jac, filling her vision. Fear blew her cold. It roared once and started to run toward her.

Jac slammed the door shut and raced down into the mirrored maze. She had turned a few times when she heard the door getting blasted off its hinges. It was coming for her.

In her panic she took a corner too sharply and

wound up bumping into a mirror, hurting her shoulder and slowing down. She stopped to check and make sure it was okay. She could already see the skin starting to discolor into what would be a huge bruise. When she looked back up at her reflection, it was smiling a dark, secretive smile at her. It was unnerving. Made even more unnerving by the fact that Jac *wasn't* smiling.

She took a step back, and her reflection took a step forward, still wearing that taut, terrible smile.

It's the House, she told herself. *It's just the House.* She squeezed her eyes shut, and when she opened them again, her reflection was pressed flat against the glass, like she was trapped inside the mirror, wearing that terrible smile, a fire burning in her eyes. Suddenly she started to grow and change, her arms stretching, her legs bending the wrong way. Jac's stomach roiled as she watched herself break and morph. Her reflection grew tall, filling in the mirror. And then, just before Jac started to run again, her reflection's jaw started to unhinge and drop so that her mouth was a giant O. From it the screaming began.

Jac stared horrified at the Mourner. *It couldn't come through the glass, right?* Jac wondered. It couldn't reach her, she thought, just as the Mourner lifted a gray hand out and her fingertips slipped through the glass like she was emerging from water, dripping and shiny. Jac turned to run, her heart like a wild thing set loose as the Mourner pulled herself out of the mirror and then quickly scaled the mirrored walls until she was on the ceiling, right above Jac, her face still contorted in a scream. Jac ran, and as she did the Mourner ran along with her, keeping pace from the ceiling.

She was terrifying, skittering along the ceiling like that, and the noise was deafening, but Jac couldn't help but notice that she wasn't coming down to attack her. She was just following her, trailing her. But for what? To test this theory, Jac did the one thing that her body and mind were telling her not to do.

She stopped.

Her heart thrumming inside her, her hands shaking, she stopped and stood as still as possible. Above her, the Mourner did the same. Jac chanced a glance up, but she still found the Mourner too terrifying to really look at.

You have to face it, the House whispered.

The Mourner was just hanging there, impossibly, from the ceiling. Jac walked backward. The Mourner skittered across the ceiling.

What is she doing? Jac wondered.

She's following you, the House said. *She wants to see where you're going.*

And it dawned on her that she must be close. She touched the key in her pocket, and when she did the Mourner stopped screaming for a moment. Yes. This was it. She was close to the cabinet, and the Mourner was going to wait and see if she could find it. She pulled the key out of her pocket, squeezed it, and headed forward. She could hear her up there, skittering along, but at least she'd stopped screaming. It was a brief respite.

She heard something else then. It was something small and light, something that danced across the air. Something that felt familiar to Jac.

She heard laughter. Not cruel laughter, but genuine. She heard a kid laughing, light and soft, like someone tapping the highest keys of a piano. It was like the voice on the phone, that one that asked if Jac was going to find her. And then behind that the frantic patter of little feet. Something caught her eye, and she looked to the left. It was quick and brief, but she saw it. Someone else was in this mirror maze.

It was a child. A girl child, in fact. And something about her laugh tugged at Jac. She glanced up at the ceiling just in time to see the Mourner skitter away, melding back into the glass. What if the Mourner was going after the girl? A coldness seeped through her. She imagined the House, just sitting there at the end of the street, waiting for whoever walked in, like a trap to be sprung. And now someone else was here. She thought about what Hazel had said about burning it down and how at the time it seemed unthinkable, but now . . . now it felt like the only good option.

The girl laughed again.

"Hello?" Jac said. "Hello? Can you hear me?"

Out of the corner of her eye she caught a snippet of dark hair and a yellow raincoat. This kid was in trouble and didn't even realize it. She was trapped in this terrible House with the Monster and the Mourner.

"Hey, kid!" she yelled. She jogged toward where she had seen her last, turning corners and coming face-to-face with nothing but her reflection over and over again. *Where did that kid go?* Jac wondered as a panic rose inside her. "Hello?" she called again. "Can you hear me?"

She heard skittering, like something tapping on the glass. She glanced to her left, looking at her reflection. After a beat, her reflection smiled, that same taut, terrible smile, and then turned away from her and walked off, vanishing around another corner. Her belly felt like it was filled with ice, watching her reflection that was not her reflection disappear. While all the rooms in the House were terrible, this one felt like the worst. It was the one that showed you that maybe you weren't you after all. Maybe you were just the reflection of someone you didn't, or couldn't, know.

"Hey, kid, can you hear me? I need you to tell me where you are. There are some, uh, things in here that are not . . . great."

The giggle bubbled up behind her, and Jac turned quickly. Again, there was nothing but her reflection. The lights overhead flickered, threatening to go dark.

"Kid?"

Jac took a cautious step forward, peering around another bend. "Kid?"

The lights flickered again, sending off a deep buzzing sound before going out completely. Jac waited for her eyes to adjust. She could barely see, but it was enough for her to spot the snatch of yellow jacket from the girl up ahead. She laughed again and turned another corner. Behind her, the mirrored hall lit up in a beam of yellow light.

The Monster, Jac thought with horror. It's going to get her. It's right there. She stopped herself from crying out and doubled back the way she'd come, creeping around another bend.

"Kid," she whispered. "Can you hear me? I need you to follow my voice."

There was a scream, brilliant and piercing, and Jac felt her stomach heave. She ran frantically now, arms outstretched, desperate to find the girl before anything else happened.

"Kid!" she yelled. "Where are you?"

Somewhere in the maze, the Monster bellowed and the glass shook.

She turned a corner and found herself in a small red room. No more mirrors. No more maze. In the center was a tall wardrobe with wide double doors. The wood was faded, the paint peeling. She recognized the wardrobe instantly. It had sat in the spare room of their old house in California. When she was a little girl, she used to climb in there all the time, hiding from her mother, passing the hours pretending that it led to the kind of magical land in books. The only difference between that wardrobe and this was that this one had a lock.

Her cabinet! She'd found her cabinet. This was her way out. Find the cabinet, reveal your truth. Do it before . . .

She heard the scream before she saw her. With fumbling fingers, she pulled the key from her pocket and slipped it into the lock.

Come on, she thought as the key refused to fit into the lock. The screaming was getting louder; the Mourner was getting closer. She took a deep breath and looked down at her hands. For the first time in a while she noticed they were not shaking. They were steady, and she held the key firmly and with purpose. She finally jammed the key into the lock and turned it. It opened just as the Mourner turned the corner. When she saw Jac and the cabinet, she ran full tilt toward her, arms and legs akimbo, skittering like a spider. Jac closed her eyes, waiting for the long-clawed hands of the Mourner to close around her throat.

Instead, the doors of the cabinet creaked open, and two hands grabbed Jac roughly and yanked her inside.

23

THE DOOR SLAMMED BEHIND HER AS THE HANDS PULLED HER DOWN, dragging her until she was sitting. It was terribly dark in the wardrobe now that the door was closed again.

"There is a crack in everything," a voice whispered in the dark. "That's how the light gets in."

"What is this?" Jac said, her voice lifting in panic. "Where am I?"

"You are in the heart of the House. And now you must leave your truth."

"Who are you?" Jac asked, her eyes straining against the darkness. She could see only snatches of whoever sat before her. Dark hair. The wide white of an eye. There was something ghostly about the figure before Jac.

A light flared, hot and bright. A single match

burned back the dark, and Jac gasped. Sitting before her, in that same yellow rain slicker, was the child that Jac had seen in the mirrored room. But it wasn't just any child.

It was her.

When she was seven years old. When everything had started to splinter and break.

"How is this possible?"

"Fear and guilt are sisters," the child said. "And they are always hungry. But they cannot be satisfied. You have to learn to stop feeding them." She took the match and touched it to a candle that sat between them. Suddenly Jac became aware of the fact that the walls to the cabinet seemed to be gone. They were still inside it, in some way, but also, they were nowhere. In a nonspace—like the very beginning of a story before any words have been written.

"Where are we?" Jac asked.

"A beginning," the girl said. "A new start for you."

"What are you?" Jac asked. She knew that she could not be really talking to her seven-year-old self. Time fell forward like dominoes, days tumbling onto each other. You can't just turn around and change directions.

The girl looked down at her hands, which were Jac's hands, and smiled. "This appearance is a reminder to you. A reminder of what you must do next."

"Are you . . . " The question sounded stupid, but Jac said it anyway. "Are you the House?"

The child before her cocked her head and smiled. It was a soft smile; the way kindness was soft.

"I am the House, but I am not the House. The House, like me, is just an appearance. You created us. You created all of it. You built the walls, Jac. You built them strong and steadfast so no one else could ever hurt you again. But that is not living. That is just existing."

"I don't understand."

"You called and I came. That is how it works."

"I didn't though."

"You did. You just don't know that you did. We have always been here, waiting and listening, and when a call comes, we answer."

"But I didn't call you." Jac squeezed her hands together. "I didn't want any of this. I just want to get out."

"Only you can let yourself out, because you built this House. You built it with hard strong walls to keep yourself safe. But that isn't what happened, is it? Because walls can't keep you safe. They can only keep you trapped. You walled yourself in with the monsters and the ghosts that you thought you were keeping out. This House is you, Jac. It is haunted because you are haunted."

"I don't want to be haunted anymore." As soon as the words left her lips Jac realized how true they were.

"Then you're ready to face what happened. You must leave behind your truth," the child said. "The paper in the library. What did it say?"

Jac squeezed her eyes shut. "Please don't."

"But this is why we are here. This is why you called me. You must face it. What did the paper say?"

"I . . . I don't know."

"You do. You just won't say it. It said you were dying. It said you were not going to survive this disease."

"Please stop," Jac said, pressing the heels of her hands over her eyes as if she could disappear into that darkness. There was a hard, hot thing that stirred and scratched at her throat.

"That paper was your diagnosis for a disease that was eating you from the inside out. It said you were going to die. You need to say it. You need to face it."

Jac shook her head and clenched her jaw as if she could keep all the words—every last one of them—inside her.

"You have spent all of this time with your back pressed against a door trying to keep the monsters out. But they were with you all along, not on the other side of the door, but inside you. But you don't have to do that anymore. You can open the door."

A tear slipped down Jac's cheek. "But we can't know what's outside."

The child before her smiled. "No, we cannot. And in not knowing you are just like everyone else who does not know what their future holds."

"But I'm not," she said. Now that she started speaking it felt like the words were never going to stop. "I'm not like everyone else because I know, and they *don't*."

"What do you know?"

"I know what it means. I know what it's like to stand on the lip of all this fear, to stare into the dark until it fills you. I know what it means to be told you're going . . . " She paused here and before she could chicken out said, "That you're going to die."

"And then . . . "

"Not . . . die."

"Yes. Because you did not die, Jac. You did not. Regardless of what the doctors said, you are here."

A sob broke loose from her, like the first stone in an avalanche. "Everyone expects you to just be happy. Everyone acts like it's over, but it doesn't feel that way. Everyone wants to sweep it under the rug as if it never happened. But it's still happening. I . . . I'm angry. I'm so very angry."

"Yes. Of course you are. You were hurt. Pain is a

scar. But a scar is also a reminder of what happened. Your anger can be a weapon. You can use it to fend off the darkness. You already used it to fend off that Monster. The one you used to dream about. The one that always chases you. You run from it—from its horns and its lamplight eyes, but what if you turned around and faced it? What if you looked at it?"

Suddenly the child's eyes started to glow like lamplights.

No, Jac thought. *Please no.*

"Just look at it. Bear witness, Jac." The child before her grew and morphed. Horns sprouted from her head, and her hands and feet turned into hard hooves. The long, raggedy fur came next. Jac squeezed her eyes shut and covered her head.

"Look at me, and see that whatever nightmare I once was to you, you survived," the Monster said, its voice now deep and smooth.

The headlight eyes were weaker, now just emitting a warm, kind light. The Monster didn't look as terrible as Jac remembered. She realized that all this time she had been running from it, she had never really looked. It was smaller and older, like a creature from a book she'd once read. The hot, hard thing in her throat stirred. The Monster morphed back into the child.

"You created the Monster. You crafted it from fear of the unknown. Fear of dying."

"Isn't that everyone's fear?" Jac asked, her voice small.

"Of course. But it is also a fact. You *are* going to die. Everything that lives will someday die. Life is precious because it comes with an end. But what if you stopped living every day like it was the end? What if you set that down?"

"I don't know how. I . . . They told my mother I was going to die. I heard her, late at night, sobbing into the pillow. I . . . caused her so much pain."

"No. A disease did," another voice said. "It was never you but the fear of losing you." From behind the child stepped a figure. She was dressed in a long veil, but this time the Mourner wasn't screaming. When she lifted the veil, the Mourner wore her mother's face. "Your mother is not this wailing woman you imagine. And you are not one of the ghosts."

The Mourner vanished, and it was just Jac and the child once again.

"You have been running from this since it happened. But if you face it, if you feel whatever you need to feel, you don't have to be afraid anymore. Nightmares thrive and feed in spaces where we do not shine the light. But that means we must face them.

Fill those dark spaces with connection and love and truth instead of fear and guilt—fear of dying and guilt about hurting her."

"Sisters," Jac whispered.

"Yes. You deserve to move on. But don't expect your anger to disappear. It won't. You have been through trauma, and trauma is elastic. It snaps back on you. When that happens, your anger will save you. Love will save you. Kindness will always save you. That is the key, Jac. That is what everyone gets."

"But . . . "

"Ask the question. It is the only way you will leave behind your truth."

The hot, hard thing in her throat stirred. She took a deep breath and felt something in her palm. When she opened it, a flat black stone lay there, and she knew it was the thing that stopped her from talking. She looked up at the child and said, "If I have already been seen . . . by the universe. If I have already been targeted with this terrible . . . Monster. Doesn't that mean something? Doesn't that mean that I'm not going to get what everyone else gets?"

The child cocked an eyebrow. She reached out and held Jac's hand. "You get the same as everyone else." She turned Jac's palm over and tracked a gentle finger over her lifeline. Jac looked down as if the answer was there. All this time, was it possible that she needed only to look at her own hands to know this awful truth?

To know if she was going to die young.

If she was going to die painfully.

"What is it?" she asked through a choked sob. "What do I get? How much time?"

"You already know the answer. It is why you called me. Say it."

Jac looked down at the stone in her hand and heard her mother's voice whispering to her. *Sometimes bravery is not all battle and bluster but instead it is gentle and looks exactly like kindness.*

And then, it washed over her like a warm wave. A truth she had always known. The secret to all this. "I get the same thing everyone else gets."

The child smiled. "Which is . . . "

"I get one lifetime."

The stone in her hand vanished.

"You have left your truth," the child said.

And she felt it then, something heavy that had been upon her lifted now, like a great bird taking flight. She felt her fear wicking away as if in her mind she turned her eyes forward instead of backward. She let herself face it.

And she let herself forgive.

She survived. She was the girl who lived. And that was a beautiful, brave thing.

"Everyone is broken in some way," the child said, "like cracked pottery mended with gold. The cracks matter. They glow. Without them the light could not get in. They are proof that broken doesn't mean without worth. They are proof that when you repair something, you don't restore it to what it once was; you remake it into something new. And now, you are remade, Jac."

Jac started to feel dizzy, like she was floating upward, and she realized suddenly she was. Everything was floating upward; the House itself was starting to disappear, the walls fading, furniture floating away, bricks unknitting. It was coming undone all around her, and she did not feel fear.

She felt free.

24

"JAAAACCCCC," A VOICE CALLED THROUGH THE DISTANCE. "CAN YOU hear me?"

She was floating somewhere, somewhere warm and safe. *Was it the House?* she wondered, before realizing she wasn't sure what that question meant. What House? She felt like she was on the verge of waking up from a long, strange dream. One in which she battled a Monster that was not a monster after all. One in which she set down something heavy. Something she had been carrying for too long. Something that had been making her arms ache. One in which she saw a crack lit with gold and it was beautiful.

"Jac?" the voice said. "I . . . I think something is happening!"

She heard a beep, steady and low.

Another voice. "Sweetheart, can you hear me? Jac, can you hear me?"

"Should I get the nurse?"

Suddenly a light, hot and white, burned her eyes. It was like staring into the sun. *The Monster*, Jac thought. *The Monster with the light in his eyes.* Confused, she couldn't quite grasp what that meant. Only that it was tied back to something big, something terrible. But something that had ended.

Then that thought also faded. Instead of floating in nothing, she could feel something. Something soft under her hand and head. Something was holding her body. The beeping sound got louder and louder. The light that was so bright softened and warmed and warped into a face.

"Jac?" Someone leaned over her. Was it her mother? "Can you hear me?"

She nodded. Or at least she thought she did. She was so confused, and the strange dream that she'd had still held her. She heard a voice inside telling her something important. Something she needed to remember.

"One lifetime," she croaked, her throat sore. "Just like everyone else."

"What does that mean?" another voice asked. Jac knew this voice; she just couldn't put a name to it.

"I don't know, Hazel. I think she's just confused."

Hazel? Yes, of course. Hazel. Her friend. Her very brave friend who'd followed her that day. Followed her into . . .

"The House," she whispered.

"What is she talking about?" Hazel asked.

"I don't know," her mother said. "I'm going to get the nurse."

The face vanished and Jac blinked again. Something slipped sideways then, and sleep took her down.

She woke. This time, fully. It took her a few minutes, glancing around the room, the white bed and the bars on the side. The IV in her arm. The oxygen tube in her nose. She was in a hospital. Why was she in a hospital?

Panic gripped her. Confused, she sat up, pulled at the tube in her nose. Another machine started beeping loudly. Was she sick?

"Jac?" Her mother woke from the armchair next to her. "Darling, are you okay?"

"I . . . what happened? Why am I in a hospital?"

"Nothing is wrong." Her mother smoothed back the hair on her forehead. "You had an accident. We're not sure what happened exactly. You've been scanned and everything is fine. But Hazel found you at the cul-de-sac. You were unconscious. I don't know if you were hit by a car or you fell off your bike or what, but you've been out for a while now."

"How long?"

"Four days."

"Am I . . . okay?"

"Yes. They did an MRI and a CT scan. Your brain is fine. You have no broken bones. I just . . . what were you doing out there, Jac? I was so scared when you didn't come home." Her mother's face crumpled. "I thought . . . I thought so many terrible things."

"I don't know what happened. I can't remember anything. I . . . carried something heavy for so long, Mom, and I think I put it down."

Her mother wiped at her cheeks and looked at her. "What does that mean?"

"I don't know." But as soon as she said it, she knew it wasn't the truth. She knew her truth. "It means . . ." Jac took a deep breath. She was scared to say these things, but she also knew she had to. She had found her truth. Now she needed to speak it. "I want some things to change, Mom."

"What things, my love?"

"The questions, Mom. The worrying."

"I . . ."

"Just please listen to me. I love you. And I know what happened when I was younger scared you more than you have ever been scared. I know that my disease changed everything. But . . . I can't keep carrying it. I lived."

"Darling, I know that." Her mother put her hands up as if to dismiss the conversation. "I know you're fine."

"Just listen to me, because I don't think you do. I lived. I want to keep living, but sometimes I trip because I'm clumsy. Sometimes a headache is just a headache."

Jac's mother nodded and dropped her head. "I . . . "

"I'm not trying to hurt you, Mom. I just . . . want to feel like a kid. 'Cause I am."

"I know that," her mom said. "You are the best kid. And being your mother is the best thing that ever happened to me. I love you so much. You know that, right? I know I worry, but it's because it's so hard to watch. Everything you went through. It was so unfair." Her mother wiped away a tear. "Going forward I will do my best to give you some more space. To just let you be. I will try to stop worrying, but it's going to be hard, because worrying is what I have been doing for five years."

"Aren't you tired?"

Jac's mom smiled. "I am. And it's almost dawn. So, let's say this is the new day. This is the new day where you and I try to be like everyone else. No more running around like the house is on fire."

"Okay," Jac said. "I would love that."

"I'm going to go let the nurse know you're up. I think they want to check some things. Hopefully we'll get out of here soon. Get you home. Hazel will be happy. He's practically been living here."

Jac smiled. "He's a good friend."

"Yes, he is. You're very lucky."

Her mother got up and then turned. "Oh, this was brought by your art teacher." Jac's mother picked up a bowl; it was glazed blue like the ocean and had gold cracks throughout. "Here's her note." She placed the bowl on Jac's lap and handed her the note.

Dear Jac,

I wanted to give you back your bowl so you can see that just because it broke once doesn't mean it's always broken. A break is a tribute to the life of an object—even a tribute to the life of a person. Life will at some point break all of us. But when we carry our breaks with pride—with kindness— we are not just repaired. We are remade. And that is a beautiful thing.

I hope you get better soon. And my door is always open if you want to talk. About anything.

About everything. Like you, I know a bit
about standing on the edge of everything and
then learning how to walk away and carry on.
Remember what I tell the class: Art saves.
Best,
Ms. Klein

She put down the letter and picked up her bowl. She smiled, her finger tracing a line over the gold, looking at where the cracks were.

Finally seeing their beauty. Finally seeing the light.

Jac went home a few hours later, and by the time school was out, Hazel was over. He told her all about how he'd found her, lying there next to her bike. How he ran to Sam Pensky's house and they called for an ambulance. How terrifying the whole thing was, though Jac couldn't help but notice he sounded more excited than terrified. It made her smile. Hazel was the hero he was always meant to be. After dinner, while her mother wrapped up the few uneaten slices of pizza, Jac and Hazel went up to her room.

"Can I ask you a question?" Jac said, staring out the window. She was looking toward the cul-de-sac. Looking for . . . something, though she wasn't quite sure what.

Hazel nodded, giving her a look. "You sure you're okay?"

"I think so."

"What happened out there?" he asked.

"That's what I was going to ask you."

"I just found you in the street. You were just lying there. I thought you were dead."

"You don't remember anything?"

Hazel shook his head. A memory flared hot and bright in Jac's mind. A key that wore her face. A House that talked to her.

It rushed back at her like a film played in reverse. She saw it all. The Mourner and the Monster and the Oubliette. The plates full of teeth. She shuddered at the nightmare she had built. A House to wall herself in with monsters.

Because that is how walls work. They don't keep you safe. They just keep you inside.

"Hazel, you were there."

"What are you talking about?"

"It's still a little fuzzy, but there was a House at the end of Juniper Drive. Right at the dead end. A House that didn't exist until it did. A House that just . . . appeared. We were there, and John was bullying you and dared me to go in, so I did."

She watched as Hazel, his brow furrowed, his

glasses sliding down his nose, listened to her. She kept talking, hoping something would trigger a memory.

"And you followed me in," she said. "You all followed me and then we . . . " She paused here because the story was fading. It was like a memory she couldn't hold on to.

Hazel gasped. "We couldn't get out! We couldn't get out. The door didn't lead back to the street, and we were trapped." He stood up and went over to the window and started to pace. "And we went down a ladder into this dark hole in the ground."

"Yes! You remember."

"But how? How did we get out?"

"I think I let you out."

"What?"

"I let you out. I knew you didn't belong there, and I let you out."

"Why didn't you get out?" Hazel asked.

"I wasn't finished. I . . . needed to finish."

"Did you?"

"Almost." Jac took a deep breath. "There's something else I have to tell you about. Something that happened when I was a kid. Something we never talked about because I didn't know how to talk about it. Sometimes something can hurt you so bad that it turns into a thing—a House, a Haunted House—and then you can't get out of it."

"What happened?"

Jac took a deep breath, and then she told Hazel the whole story. All of it. The diagnosis and the fear and the tests and the MRI that made the air horn sounds and the terrible knocking that had scared her so much when she was little. She told him about the pills and the headaches and the symptoms and how this was going to be a part of her life for good.

When she was done, he looked at her for a long time, and she wasn't sure but for a moment she thought he was going to cry. He had only one question: "Will it happen again?"

Jac smiled because that used to be her question. "I don't know. I hope not but I don't know. I guess though, in a way that makes me no different than anyone else. None of us know, right? We all just have to do what we can with what we get."

One lifetime.

"What can I do?" Hazel asked, perking up at the chance to be useful. "How can I help?"

"I don't know," Jac said.

He furrowed his brow and then said, "What if I told you that I'll be here, whenever and however you need me. If you need me to make you forget I'll be here. But I'll also be here if you need to talk. If you need someone to scream and run around the woods with. If you need someone to just sit with you and say that this really sucks."

Jac looked at Hazel for a second and then smiled. "I think I'll need all of those."

"Then I'm your guy."

25

TWO WEEKS HAD PASSED SINCE JAC WOKE UP IN THE HOSPITAL. IT WAS the night before Halloween, Gate Night, as they called it here. Jac thought that was strange. It was always Devil's Night in California, but she was starting to think East Coast people just did everything a little bit different. A little bit weirder. Except the pizza. That was still better.

She was supposed to go to Hazel's house. They were going to watch some scary movies and eat popcorn. She didn't have a costume this year. Trick-or-treating was for little kids, not seventh graders. But she did think that maybe they could just put some silly makeup on and grab a pillowcase and get just a little bit of candy.

Everyone should get a little bit of candy on Halloween, right?

She had left a little early, her mother at the door, thankfully not wringing her hands. Things were better. Lighter. The talk in the hospital had led to more talks, each one hard but somehow made easier by the last one. Like she was moving up a big staircase, each step closer to the top. She wasn't sure what was up there, but at least her mother had stopped referring to what happened as All of That or Everything You Went Through and instead used the term *diagnosis*. She actually said the word *cancer*. The more she said it, the smaller the word got. The smaller the whole thing started to feel. Still big, for sure, but smaller than a Monster.

Smaller than a Haunted House.

She waved goodbye, promising to text her mother when she got to Hazel's and again when she left his house. She mounted her bike, zipping down the driveway to the blacktop. She pedaled down Poplar, knowing exactly where she was going.

She stopped her bike at the opening of the cul-de-sac. There were the woods, dark against a darkening sky. The stars would start to wink on soon. Somewhere down the street a dog barked, raspy and harsh.

A flock of birds was startled out of the tree and flew in quick, panicked circles overhead before finally settling on some nearby wires. Everything was still then. Jac leaned on her handlebars and wondered.

There was no House emerging from the woods. She knew there wouldn't be. The House that had appeared had now disappeared. But she still needed to see for herself. She had resisted coming down here for so long because she wasn't sure if she wanted it to be there or not. The House had terrified her, that's for sure, but it had also given her so much. Besides, the House was only scary because she'd made it that way. Like it had told her, she was haunting herself. Whatever the House really was, it had helped her get free.

She pushed her bike forward, drawing those lazy circles, when her phone dinged.

You there yet?

Jac smiled. Her mother was trying.

I took the long way. I'm heading over now

Okay. Be safe. Text me when you're there.

I will

I love you

I love you too

Bye love

Jac smiled again. She really did love the way her mother ended each text like a letter. There was something adorably old-fashioned about it.

"Hey."

Jac turned around to see Sam standing near the last driveway.

"Hey," she said, turning her bike in another circle.

"What are you doing?"

Thinking. Wondering. Watching, she thought. But all she said was, "Nothing. What are you doing?"

"Listen, I . . . " Sam dug his hands into his pocket.

"Do you remember the House?" Jac blurted without meaning to.

"What? What house?" Sam said.

"Never mind. Nothing." Of course he didn't remember. He and John were barely in there. To them it would have just been a bad dream at most. Even to Hazel it was fuzzy. The House wasn't for them. It was for her. She pedaled over to Sam. "What were you going to say?"

Now that she was closer, she could see how nervous he was. Jac got that feeling in her belly again, that one that told her Sam was maybe one of the good guys.

"I just . . . I heard about . . . you."

"What does that mean?"

"I heard about what happened to you. When you were little."

"My diagnosis," Jac said. The word didn't get stuck in her throat. She smiled to herself, thinking about a stone that used to get stuck.

"Yeah. I mean . . . I'm sorry and everything."

"It's okay. I'm all right now."

"No, I know." Sam was getting increasingly more nervous, fidgeting and shifting his weight from foot to foot. "It's just . . . "

"Spit it out already, Sam," Jac said with a laugh. She circled her bike around him.

"It's about my sister. My little sister."

Jac stopped her bike. "What happened?"

"She's . . . sick. And my parents . . . aren't great. And I was wondering if you . . . " He paused again, rubbing at the back of his neck. Jac looked at him and realized that you really can't tell what is going on with a person. You think the bully at school is just a jerk, but you have no idea what he's carrying inside him. A whole tangle of experiences and feelings, hurt and laughter. People really were like their own little universes.

"I was wondering if you wanted to play video games with me," Sam finally said.

"Video games?"

"Yeah. Like you could come over to my house and we could play some games. It's her favorite thing to do, and it's the only thing that seems to cheer her up. She's eight, but sometimes, well, ever since she got sick, it's like she's five again. Always crying about things. I know it's not her fault, but I just thought maybe if you came by . . . "

Jac squinted, still unsure what Sam was asking. When it hit her, she smiled. "You want me to talk to her about being sick."

"I mean, you don't have to, but I don't know anyone else, and like I said, my parents aren't handling any of this well. With them it's all, 'It's no big deal. Don't worry.' But she is worried. I can see that. And . . . and I'm worried." His voice hitched.

"Yeah, parents think we can't handle it. Like if they don't say certain words or talk about feeling scared, then it just won't be true."

"Yes!" Sam said. "It's exactly like that. I tried talking to Lisa, that's my sister, but I don't know all the right things to say. And it's like, when I do try, I wind up just repeating the stuff my parents say. Telling her everything is going to be fine but . . . "

"You don't know if it will be."

Sam nodded, swallowing hard.

"I'd love to come over and play video games and meet Lisa."

Her phone pinged again.

"Shoot, that's my mom." She pulled it out of her pocket and started texting back quickly. "She's worried because I was supposed to be at Hazel's."

"I'm sorry. I didn't mean to get you in trouble," Sam said.

"You didn't. Smile." Jac swung an arm around Sam's shoulder and snapped a selfie with him. "I'm just going to text this to my mom, so she knows I haven't been kidnapped by bandits and everything is fine."

Sam smiled. "She seems like a cool mom."

Jac laughed. "In some ways she is." She slipped her phone back in her pocket and said, "So yeah, I would love to come by and play video games and meet Lisa."

"Thanks, Jac. Thanks a lot. And . . . I'm glad you're okay."

"Me too, Sam." There was a weird pause, and Jac could think of only one way to fill it. "I'm going over to Hazel's to watch scary movies. You want to come?"

"When?"

"Now."

"Um . . . " Sam looked up and down the street. "Sure. Let me just tell my folks."

"Cool."

She watched him run back to his house just as the

porch lights along the street all started to wink on. Jac looked at the woods and then up at the stars.

She thought about her mother's quote. About how bravery could look more like kindness than anything else. Maybe she could show that to Lisa. Show her the power of kindness.

Jac knew everyone always focused on the dying girl. But now, she knew that facing death and then learning how to live, how to breathe, how to go on, well, that was something too. Something maybe even harder than dying.

She thought about what she would say to Lisa when she met her and then decided not to plan it out. Maybe they would just play games. Maybe Lisa would have things she wanted to talk about. Maybe not. It didn't matter. All that mattered was that she would make sure Lisa saw that even when everything seemed so scary right now, that it wouldn't always be that way. She wanted Lisa to know that sometimes, unlike what some of those books and movies want you to think, sometimes the sick kid doesn't die in the end.

Sometimes she lives.

AUTHOR'S NOTE

The story you just read is Jac's story, and I am not Jac. But we share a lot in common. My story started in 2014 when I was diagnosed with breast cancer, had three surgeries, three months of radiation treatment, and then three years of hormone injections, which as of my writing this in 2021, has started again. One of the things that I learned from this experience—I do not call it a journey—is that a diagnosis changes you. You are not the person you were beforehand, but that is OKAY. You're a different person now. All our experiences, even the ones that scare us the most, make us who we are. They all add up to the person we were meant to be. And they all matter.

There are many parts of *This Appearing House* that are true, but none as true as the notion that trauma is elastic. Trauma takes time. It is a thing you learn to carry until you are ready to put it down, and that timetable is different for everyone. I wrote my fears into Jac. I wrote my worries into her. And then I wrote her an ending that she deserved. I hope if anyone reading this takes anything out of this story it is that. Ten thousand five hundred kids under the age of fifteen will be diagnosed with cancer this year. The overwhelming majority of them will survive. I wrote this story for them. Maybe you are one of them. If so, I see you and I love you.

I see the cracks filled with gold that make you glow.

ACKNOWLEDGMENTS

This book wasn't supposed to exist. It was just supposed to be a Word doc, a testament to the fact that I got sick and I lived through that storm and I used the only tool I've ever had to figure out how to go on.

I used a story.

And then Amber McBride came along and changed everything. And for that I am eternally grateful.

Thank you to my incredible agent, Rena Rossner, and to my editor, Sara Schonfeld, for believing in me. Thank you to everyone at Katherine Tegen books: Jill Amack, Mary Ann Seagren, Laura Harshberger, Mark Rifkin, David DeWitt, Joel Tippie, Sean Cavanagh, Vanessa Nuttry, Emmy Meyer, and Jacquelynn Burke. Thank you to my illustrator, Maike Plenzke.

Thank you to Amber, Aly, Liz, Kath, Linda, and Chris. Thank you to my Ride or Dies: Tomi, Jes,

Cindy, Beren, Julia, and Natiba. Special shout out to Kris, Julia's mom!

Thank you to the Grochalski family and my nieces and nephews, Nick, Neve, Annie, and Wesley. Thank you to my mom, Trish the Dish, and my amazing sisters, Stephanie and Jennifer.

Thank you to my wonderful husband, Jay. You walked through that storm with me. You're my copilot, my starship survivor, and the best member of this two-man crew.

And finally, thank you to Big Ron. You didn't get to read this one Dad, but I'd like to think you'd like it and I hope you'd have recognized all the parts that are you.

There is a poet who once said, "Which brings us back to the hero's shoulders and the gentleness that comes, not from the absence of violence, but despite the abundance of it."

You're that hero, Dad. You taught me how to weather this disease with humor, grace, and dignity because that is how you did it. Every day I try to be the kind of person you were, one who chooses kindness not because it's easy but because it's right. You made the world a better place for everyone who had the privilege to know you. And the greatest gift the universe ever gave me was that I got to be your daughter.